THE
CONNECTION

David Clark

PAGE PUBLISHING
Conneaut Lake, PA

First originally published by Page Publishing 2023

ISBN 979-8-88793-891-2 (pbk)
ISBN 979-8-88793-901-8 (digital)

Printed in the United States of America

To all victims of evil.

CHAPTER 1 INTRODUCTION

It's another warm day as I sit on my balcony of my apartment overlooking the many yachts and boats of the marina. I drink my coffee and look at the beautiful blue sky littered with candy floss clouds and finally think that global warming has found Hartlepool. The environment is changing as the world changes but as I sit here in the warmth, I am very thankful.

My name is James Fraser, I am very close to my half century of existing in this unforgiving world. I have embarked on a new career as a private detective/Investigator. It's been 2 months now since I decided on my new career path and after spending lots of my savings on expensive advertising I am beginning to wonder if it's all worthwhile. I think of how I got to this position in my life, I was born in Hartlepool, a small town in the Northeast of England. It is not an affluent town in fact it's a town that has slowly been dying. A town neglected by Governments of all colors but mainly stripped of its dignity by the blue Government. So, growing up in this town was very hard as you border on real poverty, so to prevent that you learn to fight which is normally six months after you are born. If you don't fight in this place, you get left behind and become a nobody. Fighting comes in all forms, determination to be educated so you can give yourself half a chance to escape this hell hole and to be able to physically fight, as I did. I was educated to a good standard but as I ponder my life I always regret not applying myself more in my education. My main aim growing up was to charter all my anger and aggression into being someone, so I took up boxing. However, although I had plenty of raw talent, I was not dedicated enough in the pugilistic art to learn the correct skills that you need to move up in the world of boxing. I just could not get my head round that someone in front of me wants to hurt and injure me and I wanted to literally destroy that person with pure unadulterated violence. My first few fights went well as I won them but then my trainer decided I should move up a grade to fight a very promising boxer who had won all his 10 fights in style. The guy literally boxed my head off with swift feet movements and body movements like he was a ballroom dancer. Inside my rage was exploding as I wanted to just throw the gloves off, step into his private space and tear him apart. Unfortunately, boxing is for the purists and not violent predators like me.

On returning to the dressing room my trainer said "you must learn to channel your rage and aggression into boxing with skill. Don't worry about that defeat as you will learn more from this then a scruffy win." I thought he was delusional and knew that this game was not for me, so in a strange way he was correct in what he said as I learnt from my defeat by walking away from the sport! So, I was at another crossroads in my life, what do I do to make money so I can survive. My friends who were all from backgrounds similar to me and mostly skilled in the dark arts of drug dealing, thieving, violence and gambling suggested that I should try street fighting which had become very popular in Hartlepool. They suggested that my rage and attitude was perfect to be a star in this underground sport. It was a good idea as my aim in boxing was to hurt my opponent badly but was restricted from applying this by rules and referees. So, we embarked on registering myself into this dark world which was ran by gypsies with very little rules and the moniker of last man standing wins. I wanted to watch these fights to know what to expect and it was while watching a fight I became hooked and wanted to be part of it.

This activated a period of my life which I am not very proud of as I had 9 fights losing 2 and with all my wins, I was pulled off my opponent after nearly killing him. I had become a plaything for my friends and others to gamble on and win lots of money. I also, had made lots of money and was being paid to fight. However, my last fight and loss made me realize what I had become, as I sat alone in a dressing room with my jaw dislocated, my friends had walked away from me after losing sizeable sums of money from my defeat. I was a nobody, I had no career, I was aching from head to toe, and I will be remembered for being a loser.

My life had to change, and I needed to change my outlook, plus I needed to make my parents proud whom I had made very unhappy due to my choices. My father was an ex-RAF squaddie in his teenage years, so I spoke to him about joining the forces to escape from this abyss I was being swallowed up by. My father told me to apply for a trade in the forces which would enable me to be skilled for life and embed the discipline I needed to channel my anger.

I joined the army at the proud age of 28 as a mechanic. I have always wanted to be the best at anything I have done. So being in the army gave me lots of opportunities to fulfil my ambitions. I trained very hard to a point where I was muscular but not in a competition way. I took up wrestling and became a champion then back to boxing where I became light-heavy weight army champion (yes I had learnt discipline and the ability to channel my rage). I learnt to shoot and pushed myself to become a champion at that also. In fact, I could shoot a bats ear off through a hole in a tree! Due to my name appearing at the top of leader boards I was becoming to be noticed by upper echelons in the army and I was approached to become a paratrooper. Of course, I accepted as jumping out of planes would be a tremendous adrenaline rush plus the fact the paras were an elite unit was very appealing. After 2 years of being a para and climbing to the rank of sergeant I was asked by my commanding officer if I would like to take place in the selection program to be a member of the SAS.

"Wow, to fucking right sir" was my response which got a wry smile from him. I passed the selection program and became a member of the Regiment as it was colloquially named by my colleagues. During my period in the Regiment, I was highly trained in close quarter combat and the many ways to kill another human. I was part of an eight-man unit working in 2 fours who were stationed at different parts of the world to perform reconnaissance on political enemies, drug cartels, traffickers, major gangsters, and terrorists. Our briefing was to gather as much evidence on our enemy as possible but if compromised we would be left to fend for ourselves and denied all knowledge of our existence from the British authorities. I was fine by this and reveled in the total freedom to do my job and to have carte blanche to remove scum from this earth as basically I did not exist. During this period, I had killed many people up close and through cross hairs. I had become a very skilled killing machine and had even honed my skills with learning the art of Laijutsu in my time off away from the battlefield. This is the art of mental presence and quick reaction which was very useful when in close combat with several enemies.

I really enjoyed my job, and I would quickly dispense any guilt of taking another life by instilling in my head that these people I kill are scum and the degenerates of society who prey on the good law abiding people of the world to feed their sick lives. Just one example of one of my kills was we were in a bar blending in with the natives deep in Columbia. The bar owner had two children both daughters who would help serving the customers in his bar. We were there to watch and gather evidence on a major drug cartel leader and we regularly used the bar while undercover to blend in and be classed as locals by regulars. The bar however, attracted members of the cartel who would abuse the locals and act like royalty using fear and threats to lives to make themselves very unpopular! On this occasion a member of the cartel who was very unpleasant sporting a scar from cheek to cheek decided to shoot his Kalashnikov into the ceiling shouting how connected he was and how brave he was. I had clocked my colleagues who had placed themselves in various strategic areas of the bar becoming quite alert and I had started to shake with my adrenaline racing. I was stood up with a tequila and decided to sit down which somehow offended Scarface who screamed in my direction to "ponerse de pie puta" (stand up bitch) I replied "no thanks I have just eaten" Scarface became very animated with his gang all standing and pointing their weapons in my direction. He walked towards me with his gun raised and I thought my time had come and I was about to be sent to hell, when the eldest daughter of the bar owner who was about 15 grabbed my hand and pulled me away towards the stairs of the bar. As we went up the stairs, I waited for the bullets to pierce my body but instead my ugly friend called after me to "giro de Vuelta puta" (turn around bitch). I did this and all his lackeys started laughing. He then in a terrible accent asked me "are you a pussy" with my reply "no sir I am a tiger" He looked puzzled and upset but needed to show his honor, so he grabbed the bar owners younger daughter and produced a knife placing it to her throat. This was now getting out of hand, and I needed to think quickly but not to be compromised as killing a bar full of cartel members would be too much for the British Authorities to explain away. So I grabbed the daughter who had saved my life moments earlier, drew my knife and put it to her throat looking at scar face while laughing and saying "me parezco a ti ahora puta" (I look like you now bitch") I think the bitch part went too far as he threw the daughter away shouting "eres todo mio hijo de puta" (you are all mine motherfucker) so enough of the bitch! And he walked towards me pushing people out of the way to get to me. My plan had worked, he had released the young child and I released the girl as he made his way towards me. He was now going to be part of my world but not for long…as he closed in and before he could draw his knife towards me, I had ducked under him and swiftly embedded my knife into his throat. He hit the floor jerking with his hands on my knife, his eyes wide with fear as he was about to meet his maker. I watched his life leave his eyes and heard the clicking of weapons waiting for my ending but as it never came, I looked up and saw the bar locals all aiming their weapons at the cartel members. The message was clear and the rats left with tails between their legs. I removed my knife from Scarface's throat and wiped it clean on his back while the bar owner was full of praise for me. I then turned to the girl apologizing to her after thanking her for saving my life. My colleagues were less forthcoming telling me we had to leave pronto as we were now compromised. So as I explained earlier ridding the world of dangerous parasites did not faze me at all.

For over 10 years my life was dedicated to the Regiment and keeping ordinary people safe. I have been in many dangerous situations but thanks to my training and other abilities I have survived to tell the tale. So, for the last 5 years after leaving the regiment I have tried to live an ordinary life which is very difficult as I know there are people out there hell bent on destroying this utopia. I tried being a car mechanic through my trade I earned in the Army, but I found it uninteresting, boring and very routine. This is now where I am in this stage of my life 47 and pondering what my future will become. As I sit on my balcony enjoying the warm weather while our planet is dying my phone rings.

CHAPTER 2 ROY

"Hello"

"Is that James Fraser the private investigator?"

"Yes it certainly is, whom am I speaking to please?"

"Oh, er, I thought I would get your secretary and not have a direct link to you…my name is Roy Mckray"

"Hello Roy, Yes you are very correct that it is strange to be directed to me immediately, but that is because I am still interviewing suitable candidates to be my secretary, so what can I do for you Roy?" I lied quickly.

Roy Mckray was a big fish in Hartlepool as he was a founder of the property developers M&M Builders and Property Developers, so I was eager to know what his problem was, he was also correct in expressing his shock to be able to contact me directly. I had made a lot of enemies during my time with the Regiment, which included very bad people who would love to meet me in person. I had made it very easy for those people by giving them a direct link to me. I needed to rethink that, quickly!!!.

Roy asked if I find missing persons, I said yes even those who do not want to be found.

"Who do you want me to find Roy" I used his name to make him feel like he was bonding with me.

"My wife" he said.

"Okay Roy, this is where our conversation on the phone ends as I need to meet you in person so you can tell me everything…is that ok?"

"yes of course can you come to my house and I will tell you everything I know"

He then gave me his address which only confirmed to me where he lived as I was aware of his home and the affluent area he lived in. However I was very cautious of going to his home unarmed as I mentioned earlier I have a lot of enemies and although I did not regard Roy as my enemy, He could be being manipulated by assailants to draw me out. I decided to arm myself with my Glock 9mm I had purchased from a dealer in Manchester 3 years ago. It was a quality gun designed never to jam so it was my favorite small firearm. I also carried my serrated 6 inch bush knife inside its sheath strapped to the inside of my right ankle. I was prepared for conflict but hoped for a peaceful meeting.

I drove to Roy's house parked on his drive then surveyed the surroundings for anything out of place. As I was walking towards his door, Roy had already came out to greet me, he was about my height of 1.78 meters he was very well groomed and it was clear that he kept himself in shape. However, his eyes gave away the pain he was suffering as all light had disappeared leaving just an empty space and sadness. I shook his hand and introduced myself while scanning the open door behind him. He invited me in and at no point did I think I was walking into a set-up. The guy was truly broken and walked with his shoulders slumped and head down. He directed me into his ornate study which was adorned with pictures of a very pretty foreign woman. I assumed that this was his wife. He offered me a coffee which I refused and spoke

"Let's just get down to business please Roy", I wanted to know everything and wanted to watch his eyes while he spoke to me.

"Kathy was the love of my life, she gave me the joy and happiness I had been looking for, for years, she was my world", I didn't want to interrupt, but thought this guy is a multi-millionaire and can buy, do anything he wants yet this lady had gave him the true meaning of life. I myself had purposely stayed away from a relationship with the sole reason of never putting a decent human being in danger through my work. I have never loved anybody and walked away from women who I have been entwined with for the sole purpose of keeping them alive. However, I longed for the day that I finally fell in love with someone but hopefully I was somewhere where I could never be found.

"She was originally from the Philippines, and I had met her on a dating site", Roy had continued and snapped me out of my daze.

"Okay Roy, That's fine please continue", so money cannot buy happiness, the guy used dating sites to meet women, which was no problem to me, but had Roy grew sick of Kathy, got rid of her and trying a double bluff?

"As soon as I saw her my heart beat faster and I was smitten, we met at a restaurant of my choice and we just talked like we had knew each other for years" I could see tears in Roy's eyes betraying his smile he had while describing his precious moments with Kathy.

"She was living in Indonesia with her family who had moved from the Philippines there for a better life. She had told me she had decided to come to the UK for an education and better life", This part of the story interested me as it's not cheap to fly to the UK from Indonesia, plus she needed to apply for a visa which again costs money, so how did she manage that? I had noted all this down while Roy continued.

"After meeting Kathy, we both felt for each other in the same way, and I suppose it was love at first sight. I didn't want to lose her so I invited her to live with me as I could not imagine her living anywhere else, my family were totally against the idea and indicated ridiculously that she would try to take All my money, this was ridiculous as Kathy was proud of who she was and was working 3 jobs, never asking for anything from me"

"Roy I am going to blunt with you so if I upset you just stop me…ok?" He nodded and I said,

"It's illegal to work on a visit visa in this country Roy, so how did she get these jobs?"

"Maybe I should have explained better, but after our first meeting we agreed to meet again the next day at my home. Kathy stayed the night, and I was in heaven, so I asked to marry her the next morning to which she said yes." Right so this explains the family resistance towards her, but still not her working illegally. Roy continued.

"We married on a whim in Gretna Green with no one in attendance, and we were so very happy and madly in love with each other. After the wedding I applied to the immigration to make Kathy a legal resident of our country. It was finally agreed with me spending lots of money for this to happen, but before you comment about the money, I don't really care about it and felt securing Kathy as a British citizen was worth all the money in the world" Again I made note of this and decided my rate had just doubled.

"Okay Roy so what has happened to Kathy in your opinion and why aren't the British Police involved?"

"I fear she has been kidnapped by someone to get my money, with the police they dropped their investigation saying that Kathy had probably returned to Indonesia implying she had got all she wanted from me and just left, which is total Bullshit as we were madly in love" The pain in his eyes was clear as he spoke the last sentence, but I had noted the police response which was basically Roy was a victim of a scam by Kathy. It was ridiculous as it was clear this man was deeply in love with Kathy, and I didn't doubt that this was reciprocated by Kathy as Roy although blinded by love was no idiot. I asked Roy.

"Has anyone contacted you for a ransom for Kathy?"

"No but if they do, I will pay double for her return!" My rates had just increased again.

"Right Roy I will find Kathy for you, but I need a recent picture of her, all the places she worked and her family address in Indonesia as I will need to go there." "I then told him my rates which included all flights, hotels etc. He said, "No problem James and if you find her I will give you double of what you want." Damn, I should have asked for more… Roy then collected everything I had requested handing me a picture of Kathy from the inside of his jacket pocket. I looked at it and saw that Kathy was a very pretty lady who was petite and well groomed. She had a deviant stance as she posed with a proud look on her face.

The picture meant a lot to Roy as he was very reluctant to hand it over, he then said, "please find her James and bring her home". I responded.

"Is that in any form" meaning dead or alive.

"I just want her home near me" he replied, and I watched the tears drop from his eyes. He had hope but he was no fool believing there was a chance she was already dead. The guy was truly heartbroken, and it was clear to me that Kathy had not left by her own choice. I suspected foul play and I needed to dig into Kathy's background and her life in England. I needed to find out how she got to England, how she paid for that, where she had lived before meeting Roy, I needed to meet her family, friends, where she was working her 3 jobs especially when those jobs were being performed illegally, before she had met Roy. I fear that one of those factors has got her into trouble as the love match with Roy was completely genuine. If that was not the case Kathy would have asked for an allowance from Roy and a major place on his will but she had declined this and made her own way in the world relying on her jobs which she kept working after being married, and only enjoying being treated lavishly by Roy with him by her side. I was fired up inside and determined to find Kathy as I left with calling ahead as my first port of call was the police to get their side of the story.

CHAPTER 3 DCI CROFT

While driving to the police station I thought about Roy and the pain he was going through and reflected on his love for Kathy. I had never experienced any feelings for any woman, so to see what another person whom Roy loved intensely had made him become sent shivers down my spine. Would I be fortunate or unfortunate to ever have those feelings? One of life's great mysteries I said out loud to myself. While zoning out I was totally unaware that I had reached the police station. As I entered, I spoke to a desk sergeant introducing myself, and informing him why I was there before asking to meet the officer in charge of Kathy's disappearance. He was very skeptical but called someone on the phone while I sat and waited. A door opened after I had been waiting for 30 mins and a tall well-built man in plain clothes walked towards me and introduced himself as DCI Tom Croft. I reciprocated the greeting, and he told me to follow him.

We walked to an interview room which had 2 chairs a table with fixed bars on it presumably for handcuffs, CCTV in every corner and a mirror on one wall, presumably a 2 way mirror were other officers viewed a suspects interview. Was I a suspect? I thought or is there anyone on the other side of the mirror? I spoke first,

"This is very nice, but I really thought you would have an office" waiting for his response.

"I wanted to bring you here so we could check your credentials in a safer environment" Croft replied

"I have been hired by Roy Mckray to find his missing wife, as you the police have stopped looking for her" was my reply, as I did not need to defend my credentials in my opinion, so I hit him with an accusation against the police.

"Well Mr. Fraser you are very wrong in your accusation which when I get conformation of who you are, I will spell out to you crystal clear!" I had hit a raw nerve with my accusation and his response was very defensive and intriguing.

"My credentials are fully legitimate as I am a fully licensed PI, so why don't you elaborate on your statement" I liked DCI Croft as he was a no-nonsense copper who gave the impression of a fearless man who was exceptionally good at his job.

"we wait for confirmation first Mr. Fraser"… "Please. Call me James as we do not need to be formal" I replied trying to lighten the mood,

"Ok Mr. Fraser won't be long now", as I said earlier a no-nonsense copper and now with a sarcastic sense of humor. Yes, I liked him!

The door opened and a female officer stood in the door calling Croft to her. They walked outside leaving me to stare into the mirror, which is a police tactic to unnerve suspects, so why am I being treated like a suspect?

The door opened and Croft entered with the female holding a chair. I am about to be interrogated I thought, so let's have some fun. They both sat opposite me and I looked at the female cop, in fact she didn't look like a cop as she was dressed in a pin stripe suit, her long black hair in a ponytail, and she sat bolt upright like she had a metal bar stuck to her back. She was very formal with a steely look in her eyes. She certainly was no copper, a solicitor maybe I presumed. I never spoke as I waited for them to speak next and when they did it blew me away!

"This is Stella Mathews of MI6 and she has requested to sit in on our interview, you are within your rights to have your own solicitor present, however, what will be spoken about today will not be recorded and you must sign the official secrets act, meaning you can never speak about this interview to anyone." Said Croft. My immediate thought was who really is Kathy Mckray? This case had suddenly moved from a simple disappearance to something very sinister.

CHAPTER 4 STELLA

Stella spoke next and I studied her more carefully while she spoke. Through my previous role in the Regiment, I had been part of meetings with the British Intelligent Services and throughout that time MI6 had changed from experienced field operatives to the New Age of University educated young desk operators. Stella was part of this new breed of spook.

"Let me just say that when your name was mentioned alarm bells started ringing in HQ"...she said, I was still studying her while she spoke, she had high cheekbones deep blue eyes and pursed lips that hardly moved as she spoke. She was of course attractive which she used as an advantage.

"That's nice did you also get aroused at the mention of my name" I responded. Through the corner of my eye, I noticed Croft giving a wry smile at my attempt of joviality. He seemed to be enjoying my banter. However, Stella was not and responded,

"Mr. Fraser I have been briefed about your methods and I don't approve of them or your offensive remarks"

"Well then little Miss fiery pants as the conversation is not being recorded, I can offend you as much as I like. And just for your information, my methods were fully legitimate and on the orders of the military and no doubt by the service you now work for, also those methods helped keep you safe and the ability to suckle your mother's tit while she sucked on her silver spoon on a night in your palatial home" I replied,

"You have the wrong impression of me, I don't come from a privileged background as I worked hard to get where I am, and my pants are quite cool" Touché and not even a flicker of a smile. This was getting good, but I wanted to know about Kathy, so I said,

"You now have my undivided attention so please tell me about Mrs. Mckray and why you are involved. If your pretty little ass gets any colder you can always hop over here, and I will warm it up for you" again not a facial movement but Croft could not stop smiling. I knew I liked him, and I had also warmed to frosty ass,

"If you have finished your childish comments and offensive remarks I will continue"

"My comments are genuine and honorable Stella, designed to melt your cold exterior and also to hopefully loosen your trousers!"

Croft interjected and said with his face lit up giving him away,

"Okay enough of this verbal courtship, we are here for a serious reason so please continue Stella and please Fraser keep your wit to yourself" message loud and clear, I was here for a purpose, Stella spoke next,

"MI6 are involved in this case because Kathy Marie Cuzon is a ghost, she boarded a plane from Jakarta paying for business class to Paris. However, while in Paris we lost all trace of her until she had come to our attention in the UK"

"Okay" I replied and continued "So why the interest in Kathy from MI6?"

"We have agents in Indonesia watching a certain Andre Mussalah, whom you will be aware of from your military days"…she was correct in what she said. Mussalah was the biggest drug dealer in Jakarta with connections in Mexico and Columbia. He was a big player in the export of Heroin and cocaine from the Asia region. Many years ago, my unit were sent to Jakarta to obtain information about his organization and connections. He was a particularly violent man who surrounded himself with well-trained Hench men and he was known for using innocent and inconspicuous woman as drug mules. My unit had provided the authorities with mountains of information about his organization before we were removed from that operation, so I was under the impression that Mussalah had been shut down and he was rotting away in some squalid prison in Indonesia. Apparently not, so I said,

"So Mussalah is still active which is a surprise to me, and I presume Kathy was a drug mule being used by him?"

"You presume correctly, however Mussalah was incarcerated after your team's intelligence on his organization, but he only served a minimum of 2 months in prison. He then continued with his organization becoming an even bigger name in the Asian continent as he was suspected of being connected to the Indonesian government, which you will be aware of is corrupt. He stepped up his illegal activities and used woman as drug mules on a regular basis. We of course would pass on all our intelligence to the different countries the mules were entering with lots of arrests and deaths to the women as the bags inside them burst. Mussalah is very insular and trusts only his inner circle, so he tends to use the same women as his mules, unless they have died or been arrested. We think Kathy was one of his mules who he was very close to hence the business class flight and her ability to evade arrest then arrive in the UK without our knowledge" Stella had stopped talking and I thought how Roy will digest his soul mate was part of an international drug running organization.

"So where is Kathy now and who did she deliver her goods to in the UK?" I replied

"As I said earlier Kathy is a ghost and we don't know where she is, as we presume, she has been removed from the UK the same way as she got in. As for her customer we also don't know but as she initially surfaced in Liverpool our suspicions are the Liverpool/Irish families who distribute their illegal trade on the streets of the UK. Kathy was well connected as she paid cash for everything and being a poor person from the Philippines and no job in Jakarta was very unusual."… This explained why she never asked for money from Roy as she was being funded by drug cartels. Roy will be pissed at this news or in his case destroyed. It was at this thought I had decided not to tell him about his beloved Kathy and her activities as I thought the memories, he had of her would be better than knowing about her past life. So, I asked,

"How did she end up in the northeast of England and where was she living before meeting Roy?"

"We believe Kathy was trying to make something of her life, as she enrolled into a local college called CentrePoint in this area, she had paid cash to buy herself a small apartment outside of Hartlepool and became lonely as she placed herself on dating sites, which is how Roy met her," said Stella.

"Well, you know so much about her but not where she is, I presume you have searched her apartment?"

"Yes, and nada, zilch, nothing, in fact no trace of her or anybody living there" was Croft's reply,

"Wait you said she had enrolled into college, as whom and to do what? Plus, Roy never mentioned anything to me about any college courses she was doing" I said.

Stella took over again, "We don't think she was very truthful with Roy about herself or her past, and she had enrolled into a chemistry class and informed her tutor who DCI Croft and his team had interviewed that she wanted to become a pharmacist so she could obtain work back home in Jakarta. She enrolled under her real name which is how we found her in this area." Jesus, I thought as I tried to digest this new information about Kathy, then said,

"This could all be very genuine, or she could be training to be something more sinister. Are you implying that Kathy was a big player in the drugs business, and she was honing her skills to become better at what she had become?"

"We are keeping all avenues of our investigation open as like you have said she could be just an innocent pawn in an evil man's game, or she could be on equal footing as Mussalah or even his partner!" I was trying to digest that a simple, poor woman from the Philippines had become one of the most illegal and powerful women in Asia all under the radar. I found it bizarre and unconvincing as anyone with that power would have been noticed and placed on an international wanted list before she could ever board a plane. I replied,

"I am leaning more towards the innocent pawn side and maybe when entering the UK with a bag full of money saw a way to get out from Mussalahs web and make a new life for herself, which she hit the jackpot with Roy"

"It is feasible but once you are a part of this evil activity and life, there really is only one way out, so if Mussalah got a sniff of Kathy going straight her life was slowly ticking away", Stella was correct as these evil people show no mercy to anyone especially one of their own who has turned their back on their criminal activities.

"So, you think Kathy is either dead or sitting at the top table with Mussalah and his empire?" I spoke

"We cannot make presumptions unless we find a body or as you say she appears again. We honestly do not know where she is which is how you are going to be very useful to us!"

"I work for Roy Mckray and not the British Intelligence service!" was my response.

"Calm down Mr. Fraser you will be contracted to MI6 and paid very well for your services" Stella had now become a massive pain in my ass!

"Been there and got the medal, so it's a no from me!" I replied

"I am sure you will come round to agreeing Mr. Fraser as you will be paid large sums of money and you will be keeping the people of the UK safe which you implied earlier in our conversation as if it was your ultimate duty" Stella had jumped to the top of my Things to do before I die list! And really irritated me when she pronounced my name like meester Frazerrr. She was a bitch and good at it.

"Okay" I said, "I work for Roy primarily then I will report to you, so what do you want me to do?"

"Very good James, can I call you James?"…you can call me what you want frosty pants especially when I have my knife to your throat, I thought.

"Oh yes please Ma'am, let's skip being formal and just get naked" I said sarcastically,

Without a flicker Stella said "We need you to go to Jakarta find Kathy and disrupt Musallah's modus operandi to the UK"

"You said earlier that you have agents over there so why do you want me over there, have you no confidence in them?"

"Mr. Fraser our agents are excellent operators, but we must be fully transparent and inform the Indonesian authorities that they are in their country and the reason why, so with Musallah having a contact within their government he will be well aware of who is watching him so someone like yourself who has no connection to the UK Intelligence Services will be able to go about your business under the radar freely. By that I mean legally as we do not want a trail of carnage left by yourself and something we cannot explain away so clean up after yourself...please" so I was hominem non identitas (a person of no identity) or a ghost in military slang. I was going back in time and to be honest I was buzzed.

"Stella, I can assure you that if anyone gets in my way they be dealt with in a perfectly legitimate way leaving no trail to the UK authorities. As you so eloquently said earlier, you are aware of my methods, so you will know that I leave no evidence behind! Before I take up your offer however, I am going to investigate all Kathy's movements here and I will be looking at where she worked and visiting CentrePoint College." It was Croft who spoke next,

"I can understand you wanting to do that, but we have interviewed all involved in Kathy's life and came up with nothing suspicious. Also, James any illegalities committed in my backyard by yourself will result in myself being attached to you like a rash!" DCI Croft had again made himself loud and clear, I liked him even more as he showed no fear and was forthright. However, I had no intention of committing any crimes in the UK, or ones that would be discovered! So, I replied,

"I hear you loud and clear Tom I will be on my best behavior and report everything I find back to you Sir and of course Roy"

"Good to hear James, just remember Roy cannot know everything and we also looked into Roy who came up totally clean. However, a word of warning as the head of H. R at CentrePoint is a right old bitch who will push the wrong buttons so stay calm with her, please". Stella's first facial movement happened at that moment as one of her eyebrows raised at Crofts words to me. I found his words interesting as he had investigated Roy whom I wasn't going to, viewing him as the most genuine person I have ever met. However, it was nice to know I was right, and he was clean.

"One more thing Tom, when was the last time Kathy was seen?"... Tom turned his laptop around and started a video, it was CCTV footage of Kathy stood at a bus stop outside of CentrePoint College. I watched her stand there then the camera panned away, when it returned a bus was leaving the stop which was now empty. I presumed she had boarded the bus travelling in the direction to Roy's loving arms. Tom spoke,

"We interviewed the bus driver who could not remember anybody of Kathy's description and said he really takes no notice of who gets on and off of his bus, so another dead end I am afraid" I thought Kathy was very clever in her movements and was well aware of the CCTV.

"Okay", I said "I have got what I need so can I leave now?"… Stella spoke next,

"Mr. Fraser after you have finished your business here please report to me so I can brief you before you leave for Indonesia"… Croft then spoke,

"James keep me informed about anything you find and stay above the law!"

I stood up and saluted them both before leaving.

CHAPTER 5 CENTREPOINT

My immediate aim after leaving the police station was to discover more about Kathy, where she worked and her time at CentrePoint. I also needed to speak to Roy and find out more of his life with Kathy. I needed a drink also, so I headed home for some spiced rum and ginger. My favorite rum was Old Monk which is an Indian rum rich in caramel, spicy and smooth to drink. While drinking my rum I thought about Kathy and what she had become since leaving the Philippines. Poor Roy was looking for a soul mate for love and affection and instead had fell in love with Teresa Mendoza.

I fell asleep after too many rums and with the thoughts of evil running around in my head. I woke with drumming going on in my head and a determination to start my quest to find Kathy. I called Roy ahead of meeting him in his home again. We sat in his office again and this time I accepted his offer of coffee.

I asked Roy "Did you ever visit Kathy's apartment in your early days of…courtship?"

"No and yes, she always came here, or I would pick her up from her apartment but never went in, this was my choice as she invited me in many times but I am a snob and did not want to walk into a squalid apartment and despair about how Kathy was living before meeting me"

"Okay, I can understand that, so did you know much about Kathy when you first met her… I mean did she tell you about her past?"

"Kathy had put everything I wanted to know about herself on her dating site profile, so I really wasn't interested in what she had been up to in her past life, James I live for the present not the past and beside my past life was nothing to write home about!"… That was a strange statement as Roy was a millionaire at 21, married with a daughter before he was 25, a multi-millionaire at 30, he went into politics in his early 30's running for the conservative party for the seat of Hartlepool which he failed narrowly. His only blemish was his wife had left him for another man which is not a bad thing, however I thought Roy was naïve and certainly didn't have a checkered past life!

"Roy, are you aware that Kathy had enrolled on a college course at CentrePoint?" I said,

"No, you are wrong she worked at that college along with her jobs cleaning at 2 bars on the marina"… Roy was unaware of Kathy's activities and really took no interest in them as he was so blasé in the way he spoke. Kathy was just an angel sent to him from above in his eyes and he turned a blind eye to whatever she had done or was doing. It was all irrelevant to Roy, he lived for every moment he had with Kathy.

"Okay Roy, maybe I am wrong, and you are right, but let me tell you this, you have hired me to find your wife and I will do that, but you are going to be told the truth and nothing but the truth about what I find in my search for Kathy!"

I had decided it was a pointless exercise trying to interview Roy about his wife as he was too blinded by his love for her. My next stop was her workplaces, the 2 bars. She was working illegally so how did she get the jobs and why? The first bar I stopped at was owned by Thai's. I introduced myself and told them I was looking for Kathy Mckray or Kathy Cuzon as they might know her. They told me that she had not appeared for work, and they had found out why by watching the news and seeing her face over newspapers. I asked the Thai gentleman if he knew she was illegal when he hired her, and he said yes telling me that to hire someone legally costs lots of money in the UK so they hire people cheaply who take cash in hand. I thanked them for their honesty and informed them that it's not my business to inform the authorities so carry-on trading. They seemed happy as I left and I thought Kathy's other job will be the same, knowing she was illegal but cheap to hire. I was right and after interviewing them I was at a dead end in her working life. They both told me she was an excellent worker who gave them no problems, was on time for her shifts and a very nice lady. Certainly not an example of a major drug dealer. Kathy was an enigma.

My next port of call was CentrePoint College, and I had phoned ahead telling them who I was and what I was doing then asking to speak to the head of H.R when I arrived. On arrival I was met by this very obese and ugly woman who looked like a man in drag, she/it introduced itself as Sally Nichols the head of H.R. She told me to follow her, and we ended up in her office. She was very abrupt and obnoxious as she spoke trying to talk down to me as if I was an underling. DCI Croft had been too kind in his description of this vision of excrement.

"I am looking for Kathy Mckray and I believe she was a student at your college?"

"Let me check my computer, yes she was a model student attending all her classes on time and being very prominent in her class" She-man said,

"Why did you need to check your computer to tell me that?" I replied, I disliked this thing and she thought she could play me,

"Are you always this rude to people Mr. Fraser?"

"Only to ignorant, obnoxious people like yourself!" I said, I watched her face flush as I said that and waited for a reaction,

"I think our meeting is over as I am a very busy person, with no time to waste on offensive people like you, so its goodbye Mr. Fraser!" retorted she-man

"I have more questions for you to answer before I go Ayatollah and I don't really give a fuck how busy you are!"

"Excuse me, how dare you speak to me like that, you must leave now, or I will call security"

"That would be a very bad choice, so how about I call DCI Croft and tell him you are refusing to answer my questions so let's take you down to the station under arrest then you can answer with your solicitor present"

"Are you threatening me?"

"If I threatened you Sally you should get very worried!" this woman was a dictator who got everything she wanted without question, so to be treat like how she treats others was a shock to her system.

"Ask your questions then leave Mr. Fraser" said she-man

"How did Kathy Cuzon enroll into your college when she was an illegal citizen?"

"Mr. Fraser, we do not look into the background of our students, so we were not aware she was illegal. She had a local address and she had a passport for ID which was sufficient to enroll", so if you are a terrorist or international drug dealer as long as you pay the correct fees you get trained at this college to become even better at your job, I thought.

"I take it you do your due diligence on your employees by checking their backgrounds, but not your paying clients?" you smarmy bitch I thought.

"Everyone that works here goes through the police checks necessary to work with young people, but we do not vet our students" very interesting I thought,

"Okay, I would like to speak to Kathy's teacher"

"That will be Jim Coombes and he is also the head of his department, but you cannot talk to him without a representative present!"

"Why?" I replied, "Is he incapable of answering questions?"

"No, certainly not, it's the college policy to allocate a representative in any meeting with outside bodies" very strange I thought but I will go along with her games.

"Right, I need to speak with him whenever he is free today"

"I will check the curriculum and assign a rep to sit in with your meeting" again with her 'I am in charge games!' I just played along but thought how much I would enjoy ridding this arrogant bitch from the face of this earth.

"He is free now for the next 2 hours and you will find him in room 2C, in fact I will walk you there and you can meet my colleague Annie Jenkins who will sit in with you." She walked in front of me like a wounded elephant waddling along and looking around to see if anyone was watching her so she could drown in her self-adulation. We arrived at 2C to find another very obese and even uglier woman waiting at the door, Jesus do they hand pick these fuckers or are they made to order. She-man bid me goodbye and left me with Jabba the Hut. She knocked and entered the room were a tall man with greasy black hair was stood in front of a chalk board.

"Hello, I am Jim, what can I do you for?" was his attempt at a humorous greeting, which made me want to punch a hole in his face. Jabba then spoke and I forced myself to study her, She was so ugly I could taste vomit entering my throat as I looked at her, Her hair was amazing and surely not her own, she had bright red lipstick on and she believed she was attractive and important like her boss, she-man.

"Jim, you do not have to answer any questions you find unreasonable or personal and I will be making notes of everything that is said" Jabba had spoken, and I could taste the vomit in my mouth now. I just could not look at this beast anymore. Jim who thought he was everyone's best friend said,

"Its fine Annie I will answer all of Mr. Frasers questions"

"What was Kathy Cuzon like in your class?" I asked greasy hair

"She was a star student who excelled in all her tasks, very pleasant with all the other students and she was on her way to graduating with flying colors" Interesting that he never described her as attractive. Or was I just fishing?

"Did she tell you where she was from and why she wanted to obtain a chemistry certificate?"

"She told me she was originally from the Philippines and emigrated to Indonesia with her family for a better life, and she was doing this chemistry course to become a pharmacist in Jakarta. However, after she got married here, she said that hopefully she could get a pharmacy job here as she couldn't bear to be away from her husband" said Coombes which was very interesting and indicated she had not left the UK or not left by choice. Coombes was very confident when talking and I noticed his breath smelled of shit.

"Did Kathy have a close friend in her class?" I said and walked to the back of the class away from Coombes shit breath.

"All the students in the class were really close and friendly with each other but I wouldn't say she was close to anyone in particular" I had heard enough and was about to wrap up and go when Jabba spoke,

"I think you are finished now Mr. Fraser as Jim will be starting his next class soon and I have work to do"

"I decide when I have finished Jabba and one question for you…is that your real hair or are you wearing it for a bet?" her face flushed and I felt really nauseous, but satisfied, so I left before I vomited all over Jabba. As Croft had said, I had learnt nothing new there apart from the college was ran by monstrous megalomaniac women, and I could not understand any sane man wanting to work for those people.

Kathy was an enigma in my mind and a total mystery. What was her real reason for enrolling in the college, was it because she wanted a new life back home or was it part of her role in the cartel, did it all change when she met Roy or was that a ruse to look legitimate. I think Stella was maybe right and my answers will all be revealed in Indonesia.

CHAPTER 6 BRIEFING

I had contacted Stella for my briefing with her and she told she would meet me in the police station in the same interview room. I arrived before her so asked for DCI Croft who escorted me to the interview room and then left. I sat staring at the mirror knowing Stella was the other side making me wait. I poked my tongue out several times to relieve my boredom and after what seemed an hour the door opened with Stella entering with a man I vaguely recognized, Stella spoke,

"Apologies for being late but we hit some traffic on the motorway" so the room next door to this room must have crowds in the corridor preventing a clear passage I thought. The tall man spoke next,

"Hi James, do you remember me?" I had vaguely recognized him but could not put a name to him or who he was,

"No" then "please don't apologize Stella, everything is fine" her finely styled eyebrows raised before settling again on her stony face.

"I am Chief of Operations at MI6 Peter Wallace, we have met several times in the distant past" said the tall man, and I instantly recognized him Peter, was ex Regiment, but he was top brass. However, he was very good at his role and gained and kept the respect of the squadron. In my book he was a top bloke. He left the regiment to join MI6 and with his background quickly rose in importance. When we were ordered into active duty, Peter was our man to brief us. He was meticulous and extremely accurate in his briefings so I was glad he was in this room. I also now believed that they were genuinely late and I had been poking my tongue out at myself in the mirror!

"Yes sir I recognize you now and it's a pleasure to see you again"… I said as Stella's sculptured eyebrows moved again,

"I have been made aware by Miss Mathews that you are willing to offer your services to fight the good fight hand in hand with us. I know you won't be a paid up official member of the intelligence services but you will be a handsomely rewarded contractor with invaluable experience and knowledge and I personally am pleased to welcome you back on board"…no fucking about with Peter, straight to the point and precise. I looked at Stella and she had cracked a smile while looking at me…those icy pants are melting as we speak.

"Yes sir, but my main aim is to find Kathy Mckray first then I deal with Mussalah who seems connected to Kathy so it could be two birds with one stone" I said. It was Stella who spoke next,

"As I mentioned before James we cannot have you going rogue killing all and sundry as we cannot be seen as a murderous country on other people's turf" she now seemed almost human as she spoke with a warm glow to her face

"Well Stella, We have done it many times and left without a trace, so what are you proposing for me to do?" I pondered and waited for the answer, Peter spoke next,

"You need to remember you are not with a unit and alone so discretion is the word of the day"…which was a clear message to resist in my killings,

"We need you to disrupts Mussalah's distribution to these shores and off course bring Kathy home for questioning" said Stella who was proving herself to be a big player in MI6 and I was impressed, with James junior also impressed as he started his stretching exercises.

"Just cause enough mayhem to slow down Mussalah's operation and if he is in your crosshairs and it can be cleaned up take the bastard out!" said Peter with Stella getting extremely animated at those words, in fact I think she wanted to leave the room or even not be there, poor little darling. Peter had spelt it out to me loud and clear that I had a free reign to disrupt and execute without prejudice. Stella was moving uncomfortably in her chair when she eventually spoke,

"James that's all well and good but please let that be your final option and lean on the side of discretion, we really do not want a diplomatic incident with Indonesia who are funded heavily by China if you understand what I mean" I did and I was impressed by Stella's obvious high standing in the intelligent service, plus she had shown real balls to counteract her boss. James Junior was really stretching now when Stella spoke again,

"when you land in Jakarta you will be met by our lead operator Charlie Mcall, He will know who you are and introduce himself before getting you safely hidden" Unfortunately for Stella and Charlie I will be making other plans for my arrival into Jakarta. I replied,

"Sounds like a plan Stella so I will look forward to meeting with Charlie"... To which Wallace gave a wry grin and understood what I was going to be doing. From that moment Stella produced a file on Mussalah with pictures and details of his trusted men. There was also a document dedicated to Kathy which I would read and digest before burning. Stella continued to brief me about my mission but I had zoned out as I thought what she would be like in a nice warm bed with me and junior. I came out of my trance when Stella said,

"Good luck James and stay safe" Junior was now almost at full strength and I wondered if it was visible, but I think not as Stella stood with Peter turned and walked out of the room. Junior was distraught, returning sharply to his limp mode. So, I thought I need to pack before catching a flight to Singapore to see an old friend.

CHAPTER 7 SINGAPORE

After my briefing with Stella and Peter I had no intention of flying direct to Jakarta. I was not meeting Charlie Mcall in an airport, I will find him when I want to and it won't be in view of Mussalah's people. If Mussalah has been made aware he is being watched, then I can guarantee he knows who they are, and he will be watching them. So, I will not be walking into a camera lens when meeting Mcall. I will arrive when I am ready, and it will not be at Soerkano-Hatta Airport which is Jakarta's main international airport. Besides I need to meet an old friend who will help me with some things I need. Before leaving I buy three burner phones and remove the sim from my main phone which will be turned off and remain off until I arrive in Jakarta. I had excellent knowledge of Jakarta from my many times we were over there, providing intelligence information on Mussalah and his connections for the spooks at MI6 and for the Indonesian Intelligence services known as the BIN (Badan Inteligen Negara). It was a city that never slept, full of pollution and lots of traffic causing the pollution. It is a city split into many areas with most areas affluent in the center surrounded by poverty on the outskirts. I liked my time in Jakarta and always considered that the city contained the most beautiful women in the world. It also had an underbelly of crime and corruption filled with gangs vying with scumbags like Mussalah to profit from misery while rubbing shoulders with influential members of the Jakarta elite in complete openness of the general public. I was looking forward to being reacquainted with it again.

Before all that I needed to go to Singapore so as I boarded the plane making way to my business class seat on Emirates Airline, I thought about Angus Stewart, my colleague in my Regiment unit whom I would be meeting. Angus or Gus was from the blue half of

Glasgow in Scotland. He was a tough guy who was extremely intelligent, before he joined the army, he was an IT expert dealing with stock markets and banks. He told me that he left that job because it had become boring being a keyboard warrior as he wanted to look into his enemy's eyes, not ever seeing them through a black screen. When he joined the Regiment, I was immediately drawn to him as he was a carbon copy of myself, hard as iron and full of anger, although he would use the word fuck in every sentence. I knew he had moved to Singapore in search of riches and women. It will be interesting to see him again. It was going to be a good few hours' flight so I needed some rum and sleep. I dreamt about Stella and how angry she would be now not knowing where I was and what I was up to. I thought she would curse then apologize to nothing, but fresh air then put more make up on while staring in the mirror. She was a good girl, I liked her…at times and I would contact her when I get my new sim when in Jakarta, until that time she will have to keep drinking her Pims and biting her nails.

On arrival in Singapore and exiting passport control I headed for a phone shop buying a few sim cards and more burner phones. I had booked into a hotel on Orchard Road. I had been to Singapore many times in the past on operations mainly involving intelligence missions on international gangsters who were using this International banking area to launder money. Singapore was a beautiful place, the cleanest and meticulous organized metropolis I had been to, and it was home to many millionaires who made use of the lavish stores and shops stationed on Orchard Road. It was also home to many millionaire expats from around the world who made use of the lavish areas of the city, the plush houses, the fantastic restaurants, exceptional schools, and they chose to live in a place with a high cost of living but very low crime rates.

I was puzzled to why and how Gus chose here and could afford to live here. I called him and he answered with his broad Scottish accent "hey the fuck is thas?"

"Nice, Gus, it's your old mate Fraze"… I said.,

"fah fucks sake what a ya daying in Singapore?"

"I am going to ask the same question of you my friend when I see you"

"cum here now ya mad Geordie bastard"… Gus said then gave me his address and I discarded the phone breaking the sim card and throwing it in the trash. It was close to my hotel so I wanted a shower and change of clothes before meeting Gus. I also knew that meeting up with Gus would involve lots of drinking and reminiscing, so I wanted to be prepared. I got a taxi asking for my hotel and looked out at this beautiful city with the Marina Towers dominating the skyline. The roads so clean with drivers respectable of each other, a rarity in Asian countries. We passed Clarkes Quay and many colonial homes and buildings as this was once in the hands of Great Britain. We had entered Orchard Road and I could see from my hotel, the infamous Orchard Towers or Four Floors of Whores as it's more famously known as. It is a legal establishment that is home to bars, massage parlors and karaoke joints on four levels with the higher you climb the more expensive the whores are. My unit had frequented it many times while on mission with girls from all over the world working the floors. However, I would not be visiting this time while here, I was on a schedule which meant no time to party, unfortunately.

After checking in and refreshing myself I walked to where Gus was living as it was close. The temperature was a sticky 80c and the sun was beating down, it was very hot and on arrival at Gus's home I was damp from sweating. I looked at his pad and thought 'he must have robbed someone to own this. It was huge with pillars beside the door, three floors high and a huge garage attached to the main building. It was extremely palatial and not somewhere I would expect someone like Gus to live. I was astonished at the lavishness as I rang the bell I had also noted the CCTV camera above the door, Gus will know I am here.

The door opened and Gus stood there, with his arms open wide, he said "cum ere and give yah best mate a big fucking hug"… we hugged then entered a very ornate reception hall with a balcony staircase leading up to bedrooms I presumed. I said "we never earned that much while in the squadron to afford something like this, so who did you rob?"

"Ha Ha, straight to the fucking point as normal Fraze, let's get a rum and I will explain"…this is going to be good I thought.

"After leaving the Regiment I returned ta Glasgee and soon got bored with regular life so I decided to make some money by gambling on stocks, shares and crypto currency. After registering with this 'legitimate company' their words, I was called by an upper class English guy who informed me that with his help he would make me lots of money. He was a scammer of course with the whole company and web site totally fake and one big scam. I informed him that if he fucks off with my money, I would spend the rest of my life looking for him then I would fucking dismember him when I found him"… this is going to end bad for someone I thought.

"He was a smarmy bastard who thought he was untouchable and could hide behind his well-protected VPN. However, everyone leaves a fucking footprint and all I needed to do was find it which I was quite capable of doing. The thing is Fraze these fuckers are now worse than terrorists as they cause misery to ordinary folk who are looking to make money to keep themselves afloat, but these vermin are exploiting their weakness and scamming them out of millions and millions of dollars. Some of these fuckers are linked to terrorists, people traffickers, gun runners and gangsters while some like my 'investor' are just downright fucking scum who laugh at the people they scam. It is a crime that should be classed in the same breath as terrorism as its practiced on a massive scale by fucking vermin from Serbia, Italy, Nigeria, Australia, The UK & USA, Cyprus, Turkey and here in Singapore. I found my investor and this is where he lived, on the most prestigious road in Singapore, Nassim Road!"…… Gus used the past tense to describe his investor, so I knew he was exterminated, so I let Gus carry on.

"I watched the fucker for weeks he was a slimy piece of shit with a wife and son and he went about his business with his head held high the fucking scummy bastard. I wanted to cut his fucking ugly head off every time I watched him. Anyway his day of destiny came and I moved in, I attacked him at his front door by smashing the palm of my hand onto the bridge of his nose, he went down screaming as I walked in shutting the day behind me. He was now in my world and not as confident as he fucking was on the phone. I grabbed him by the throat with his broken nose bleeding profusely and said where your office fucker is. He led me to this"... Gus took me to a room which on entry had 4 massive computer screens nestled on a desk in the middle of the room.

"Wow", I eventually said,

"Yup, the greasy fucker had more sophisticated equipment then fucking NASA! I told him to open everything up plus his bank account, he was obliged as I had my Glock rested on his temple. The bastard started to cry saying he was sorry and please don't hurt my family. I said it had never bothered you that you had destroyed thousands of families with some of his victims ending their own lives. Fucking piece of shit, I wanted to slit his throat at that moment, but I wanted to make him suffer like he had done to thousands."......oh dear I thought but let Gus continue.

"I made him send my money back into my account with some interest, and the slimy fucker had details on everyone he had scammed so I made him send money to all those people who had suffered. He was begging for mercy which I had abandoned years ago. I told him he was going to watch his family die before I dismembered him. One last thing I told him to sign this house over to me as he will not be needing it anymore. The fucker started making demands saying if I leave his family alone then he will give me everything. I told him I don't negotiate with terrorists; I am taking everything and you are all going to die. Again, he wept like a baby, so I tied him up and gagged him while I prepared the garage for my defining act. I knew his family were out and an approximate time they would be home. When they arrived, I knocked them both out and dragged them to the garage where I had 2 nooses waiting for them. I placed the nooses round their necks and waited till they came round, I then stood them both on chairs."...... I listened to Gus and thought that he was not boasting about this but he was confessing to rid himself of the demons that had entered his head, I let him continue,

"His wife pleaded for her son's life, but as I see it his fucking son was his protégé and he would take over the family business when his slimy father had perished I wanted to cut the tree down then poison the roots. So he was going first for both mammy and daddy to watch and feel the pain they had caused thousands. I gagged them both before going for fucking slimy bastard. I dragged him into the garage sat him down in the remaining chair tied him up and let him watch his son die. I kicked the chair away and he swung while jerking away. The parents were distraught and crying but I felt nothing but hatred for that fucking slimy bastard. His wife was next, and I asked him how it all felt but he was totally distraught and pleaded for me to kill him which I did by slitting his throat, so now I was very rich and a proud owner of this fucking house. Plus, I had sophisticated equipment to find other scammers and end their illegal, disgusting businesses. I also had to get rid of the bodies, so I had a nice burning in the rear garden, shoveling their remains in a trash sack and putting them where they belong with the garbage. So, I have now been here 4 years disrupting seedy scammers all over the world, and I love this city."... Jesus I thought, Gus has turned into Robin Hood!

"I am here for a favor and know you are the man for it"... I said as I wanted to take his thoughts away from the carnage in his head.

"Anything for you Fraze what do you need?"...... I told him the full story and how I was hired by Roy before being ambushed by MI6 and my full plan mentioning Mussalah.

He replied "Mussalah the ular" meaning snake, I had forgot we called him that when watching him. The reason was because he always looked like his skin was wet and when he spoke his tongue would come out of his mouth. Gus spoke again

"I want in!"...unfortunately mate I can't include you in Jakarta but if that equipment in there can find me anything regarding The Ular's business we are back in business my old friend. But for now I just want a few passports and a contact in Jakarta for some guns and you here finding the snakes contacts and distribution centers for me...

"Fuck off Fraze I want to be part of the real action" Sorry mate not this time I have to be alone for this but I promise you we will happen again.

"Don't ever break that promise and remember I am always here if you need me in the field"...... I really hope I don't need you I thought, then said,

"Right get the fucking rum flowing I am gagging here as my throat thinks my mouth has been sewn up!"

After a few drinks we decided to go for something to eat. With my favorite food Indian, we decided on a lovely restaurant on Cuppage Terrace called The Curry Culture. It was a popular haunt for us many moons ago when we were all here on a mission. It was also just a brief walk away through Orchard Road or under Orchard Road as Singapore also had an underground city built around the metro line. It was also cooler down there which was a relief as the humidity had got worse as the night arrived. We had a fantastic meal and some beers reminiscing about the good old days when Gus announced he was ready for his bed and was getting a cab home. I was also feeling the effects of the jet lag but decided to walk back to my hotel so I could get some fresh air into my lungs.

As I walked I realized I was on the side of the road were the Four Floors are located, so I expected some attention from the whores that ply their trade outside the Four Floors. As I was approaching, I saw a large crowd outside the Four Floors and I also saw this vision of beauty outside the Irish Sports Bar nearby. As I got closer she saw me and made a beeline for me, she was beautiful with short shaggy brown hair, had olive skin and was wearing a lacy white dress that clung to her every curve. She said,

"Hi handsome, would you like to fuck me?" in a foreign accent

"Is that a trick question?" I replied

"What? I can promise you that I will make you cum many times" she announced

"I bet you can my dear" I said

"We can go to your place or I have a little place of my own we can go to, your choice, either way you are going to have the best night of your life!"

"Well to be honest, I have had a very good night tonight and now I am very tired so I need to sleep" I said with a hint of regret,

"I am from Uruguay and I bet you have never fucked anyone from there before, so come on handsome lets have some fun" she said in her sexy foreign accent,

"Well a long time ago I was in South America having sex with a lady like yourself and I kept asking her where are you from which she kept on saying you are a huge guy, so I took it she was from Uruguay" I said in my attempt to humor her, however, she responded with,

"What? I am not very good at English so cannot understand you, what are you saying?"

"Forget it, it was stupid anyway"

"My name is Christobel and people call me Christy, I will give you cheap rates as you are very handsome" she said

"Pleased to meet you Christy you are indeed gorgeous, I am Alan" I lied, but I was getting an emotional draw to this girl like a father type emotion not sexual, I liked Christy and wanted to just wrap her up and take her away from the seedy world she was in. I was also attracted to her accent and really wanted to talk more with her to get to know her more, so I said

"Would you like to have a drink with me, I will pay you for your time?"

"We can have a drink in your room before we have sex" she said suggestively,

"Christy just let's have a drink in here and talk please" as I pointed at the Sports bar.

"Okay, but you pay me full rate for fuck" she said in a disappointing way,

"Right what do you want to drink?"

"A Singapore Sling" she responded, and we went inside. I was being delusional as I thought I could change her by talking with her as I felt that emotional pull towards her. I thought of the movie Pretty Woman when Richard Gere's character had fell for a prostitute played by Julia Roberts but this was different, I wanted to help her and save her from destroying herself. She found herself a table with all male heads turning to her direction, I felt my stomach knot and I had an urge to hurt everyone looking at her. What is going on in my head I thought? I got myself a rum and ginger with Christy's drink and as I walked towards her, I could see indeed she was very attractive. We talked for over an hour and her drinks were not cheap, but she was intelligent and very open about her life. I told her I was a private Investigator looking for a missing woman which she described as 'cool'. As I tired, I told her I would get her a cab so she can go home, to which she replied

"Why don't you want to fuck me? Do you not like me?"

"No Christy I think you are very attractive but tonight I need to be alone" I responded, not indicating that I was drawn to her for other reasons. She told me I owed her $150 dollars plus the cab fare…she was very streetwise, and I found humorous. I gave her the money with pleasure walked her outside and left her looking for a cab or so I thought, as after a few seconds walking and hitting the crowd of punters outside the Four Floors, I looked back towards Christy and she was talking to a man. Well, I tried I thought and failed. I needed to sleep as my flight to Jakarta was approaching fast. I slept as soon as my head hit the pillow and I dreamt of Christy as a normal loving girl with a good job, happy in her life and me being a huge part of her life. I awoke shaking the thoughts out of my head as I would probably never see Christy again. I showered and got ready for Jakarta when my bedside phone rang. It was the reception telling me I had a package waiting for me. Gus had got the false passports sorted and left them for me to pick up. I really wanted Gus with me but could not risk the wrath of Stella and Peter plus a diplomatic incident between 2 countries as carnage would ensue with us two back together. Gus would infiltrate Mussalahs operation from his office and then supply me with all the information I needed to disrupt his supply lines. I picked the first passport from the package; I was now called Alan Shearer who incidentally is one of the greatest footballers ever to play for England and the team I support Newcastle United. I had booked a flight direct to Halim Airport in South Jakarta. This airport was primarily for domestic flights so I would just blend in with the natives. I passed through passport control with no problem, good old Gus I thought. I boarded the plane and was ready to go back to an old stomping ground of Jakarta. In Just over 2 hrs I would be back in that sprawling metropolis.

CHAPTER 8 JAKARTA

I arrived at Halim airport in South Jakarta and I had booked into The Ascott Suites in the Sudirman area of Jakarta. We had used this hotel many times while on operations many years ago. We also had continually moved from hotel to hotel in different areas for the simple reason of not being identified and making it easy for our enemies to find us. I also planned to do the same thing and keep moving around Jakarta. The first thing I needed to do was call Stella and wait for her wrath towards me.

I called Stella with a phone that I would use while in Jakarta so if I got into any trouble MI6 could locate me.

"Hello, who is this?" Said Stella after the first ring. Charming I thought,

"It's James how you doing Stella?" I responded

"Where the fuck have you been James?" Stella retorted. I wonder who taught her how to curse.

"Stella I am here in Jakarta now as I got here my way and not being advertised as you had planned!" I retaliated

"We thought you had blew us out or even worse been abducted" she replied with a touch of concern in her voice. I was feeling wanted, but replied

"If Charlie was known to be watching Mussalah, then he would have been informed and be watching Charlie. So, meeting Charlie in the airport was not a good plan for me as being a ghost I do not like being photographed by my enemy. Give me Charlie's contact details and I will arrange to meet him away from prying eyes" the next voice on the phone was Wallace and he said

"Okay James, very good and I totally agree with you but please do not go off the grid without informing us again. It's dangerous for our agents and it could give us a reason to upset the Indonesian Authorities" fair enough I thought but replied with

"I hear you Peter but primarily I am hired to find a missing woman and I will do that my way, the job with yourselves is in hand as I speak, and I will complete that as you know. I will of course keep you updated and informed of everything I will do, I lied, but first I need to meet Charlie to extract all his information on Mussalah"

"I understand James but when you do go rogue do not leave a trail of bodies for us to explain away, Charlie is an excellent operator as you will find when you meet him, he has a dossier on Mussalah and his local contacts so listen to what he tells you, remember we need you to disrupt Mussalah's operation which does not mean exterminate him, keep him alive for now.! Right, I will leave you in the very capable hands of Stella as I have a meeting to attend, stay safe James and come back to us, please" loud and clear from a man I totally respect, however how does he know Stella's hands are capable? Is that why Stella sits at the top table or am I being stupid? I pictured Stella's hands cupping Peters balls and was broken from my trance by the lady herself,

"I have sent you Charlies contact details and I will also contact him to let him know you are fine and will be in touch very soon and James I echo Peter Wallace's words 'Stay Safe'" again with the concern, maybe she likes me in a sexual way, very interesting, I respond with,

"No problem Stella, I appreciate your concern but I aren't planning on dying anytime soon!" the phone hung up, without even a goodbye kiss.

I was planning on calling Charlie and meeting with him in the Kuningan area of Jakarta which is very upmarket with high class hotels, bars and restaurants frequented by affluent locals and foreigners/expats. There was a bar we frequented when on operations called Jack Sparrow. It had a good band, good food, dark corners and lots of beautiful women. I called Charlie who seemed pleasant enough and arranged to meet him at bar around 8pm. I got in there early to have some food and situate myself in a dark booth watching the door.

I noticed lots of beautiful girls in the bar all enjoying them-selves and I had scanned the full bar looking for anyone I thought as suspicious. Nothing was standing out to me, so I thought it was an excellent choice for a meeting. I then noticed this truly beautiful, stunning girl who was with a group of friends. My heart skipped a few beats as I studied her, she was about 5ft 5inches tall, had long curly brown hair, her eyes where stunning as they drew your full soul into her, she had olive skin, a small nose and distinctive cheek bones, she was wearing a frilly red dress which emphasized her curves and she was truly gorgeous. I was mesmerized by her and was staring intently at her when a tall blond well-built man had stepped in my view. I looked at him and stood up saying,

"You must be Charlie?"

"I am indeed, and you are definitely James", he responded in his cut glass English accent. He was a Southerner as we up north of England would call him, he had an accent that the Americans think all English people speak, like, Dick Van Dyke when he was in the film Mary Poppins. He was about 6ft 1inch, with short blond hair, he was well manicured, and ladies would say he was very handsome. I told him to sit down, and I ordered 2 beers while I watched the door for anybody, I thought was following Charlie.

"Nice venue", Charlie said

"Yes it became a favorite of mine many years ago and it hasn't changed much since then"… I replied

"I waited at the airport for you for hours and thought I had missed you"

"Apologies for that, but I did not want to advertise my arrival", I replied

"So, you think I am being followed?" responded Charlie

"I think you have been but going to an airport and meeting a mystery man would send up Red Flags to Mussalah, and I did not want to be scrutinized by that slimy snake before I got prepared. If he seen me again in his vicinity, he would have recognized me as the man meeting with the MI6 agent watching him, I couldn't afford for that to happen". Was my reply. Charlie nodded in agreement and said that he was very careful in his duties and was sure he wasn't being followed.

"From my past experience with The Ular, he has eyes everywhere so he would have initially followed you then placed his eyes strategically to every area you frequented. He is a devious bastard with lackeys fanning him wherever he goes" I said

"The Ular means snake if I am correct?" Charlie responded

"It certainly does, we called him that because he always looked like his skin was wet and his tongue would poke out of his mouth when he spoke" to which Charlie laughed and nodded his head in agreement. I liked Charlie. He then spoke saying,

"Right you need to know about Mussalah and were he mostly frequents, he surrounds himself with goons and unpleasant girls, he also is very well acquainted to Liam Harper of Naylor & Harper the Shipping Conglomerates and owner of the Top Gun Bar in Blok M. It's a seedy bar full of prostitutes that Mussalah feels safe in as he sits in company with Harper, Diplomats, other dealers and a particular disgusting Englishman called Daz Stones. This guy is Mussalahs chief lackey and is believed to be a violent pedophile. Daz himself is always with a local girl who supplies young children for his disgusting habits. Blok M is a terrible place to be on a night as it's full of dangerous people and whores with lots of diseases including aids. It's in an area near to Kemang which is a haunt for expats of all nationalities and much nicer than Blok M". Top Gun was a bar we had visited many years ago while watching Mussalah, we called it the Star Wars Café. So, it looks like old habits don't die then. Harper and Stones where very interesting to me but strangely no mention of Naylor at the top table, so I asked Charlie,

"You mentioned Naylor but nothing about him, why?"

"He is a ghost and never been seen for years, he apparently is the brains behind N & H with lots of high-flying contacts including Government figures. He is never seen in public but controls Harper like a puppeteer. We have nothing on him, so we concentrate on Mussalah." Replied Charlie. I thought that maybe Naylor was Mussalahs right hand man with the contacts he was rumored to keep. All the time that Charlie was speaking to me I was looking at

Miss World and her movements she was interesting me very much as my heart was beating faster as I looked. Charlie had noticed this and must have thought I had grown tired of his conversation as he said

"Right James we must be finished so let's wrap this up by you telling me what the plan is"

"The plan is I find Kathy Mckray or find out where she is then we go after Mussalah so I will spend a few days in Jakarta visiting Kathy's family and friends before contacting you to execute my plan for Mussalah, so in the meantime do not change any routines and continue as normal until I contact you"" was my response, which got a hard stare from Charlie then a nod and finally,

"Okay James I understand, but I will have to report back to Ms. Mathews"

"Who the fuck is that?" I spoke

"Oh sorry, it's Stella to you but she is my boss". Well, well Stella was directing the traffic here in Indonesia and high up in the Intelligence agency, so I was right about her and it made sense for her to be worried about my actions in her chosen area.

"So little Miss fiery pants is your boss…good luck with that" I commented which drew a large smile from Charlie. Charlie said that he was leaving as he had business to attend to, I also had business to attend to, but it remained in here. We bid farewell until we meet again.

I watched him leave then turned my attention to Miss World. She was with friends but sat alone so I made my way over to speak to this vision of beauty.

"Hi gorgeous is anyone sitting next to you or can I please" was my opening gambit. A right old romantic I was, she looked at me and smiled which nearly made my heart burst, I was starting to shake as she said,

"Hi, please sit down" shit I was now shaking with fear and my hands had gone cold. I looked at her close up and she was beautiful in every sense, I noticed her skin was so smooth and pure and she had full perfectly formed lips that I wanted to kiss right now, but instead I said,

"My name is Alan Shearer and I am English"

"Oh, nice name and I like Englishmen as they are very romantic, my name is Putri Isna (pronounced Ishna) Delishus" she responded. I thought it was her lucky night as I was now going to be the most romantic English man she had ever met,

"Delishus eh, I bet you are!" was my attempt at a humorous response, to which she laughed and said,

"You are very handsome and funny" It's my lucky night and I have just won every lottery in the world I thought.

"Why thank you and you are very stunning if I may say so, how old are you and what is your job?" I said with my voice shaking.

"I am 35 and I have my own PR business." Was Miss Delishus's response. The ice was broken, and we talked some more each asking questions about each other and I felt myself being totally captivated by this lady with my heart beating faster constantly. I think I had fell in love finally. I found her amazing, interesting and of course beautiful I wanted to pick her up put her on a white horse and ride off into the sunset with her. She asked me where I was staying and when I told her where she just said

"Very nice hotel" I was massively disappointed and never tried any humorous reply, but said

"Would you like to have dinner with me tomorrow night?" I held my breath for her response which was,

"I would love to so where do you plan on taking me" To heaven and back many times I thought, but replied with,

"There is a lovely restaurant just around the corner called Loewy's, which has a very good reputation" I had read about it online

"OH fantastic it's my favorite thank you very much James" Yesssss, I thought, then arranged to meet at 8pm the next night inside, which was my choice as I felt a massive urge to protect Putri and keep her away from harm. I bid her farewell saying I was suffering from jetlag, and she kissed me briefly on the lips which made my legs buckle and my heartbeat faster. I left floating out the door and wondered is this how Roy had felt when he had met Kathy? If it was it gave me a greater understanding of his feelings now without her as I thought Putri was my soul mate and someone I could not live without even at an early stage of our relationship. I caught a cab back to my hotel, went back to my room climbed into bed and slept a deep sleep dreaming about Miss Delishus and how she was about to change my life forever.

I was woken by a phone ringing, it was light outside and when I looked at my watch I had slept a solid 10 hrs. I looked at my phone not recognizing the number and answered

"Hello, who is this?"

"It's only been about 36 hrs. And you have fucking forgotten about me already!" was the response from an angry Scotsman, it was Gus.

"What have you got for me big man?" I replied

"I have found Mussalah's fucking distribution depot at Ancol Port, it's owned by a Steve Naylor who owns a shipping company, which is very appropriate. I am trying to break into both Mussalah's and Naylor's computers to get more information about them. They have some very good protection on their computers but it won't keep me out the pair of fuckers, it will take time but I will get in." so Charlie was right about Naylor and it seems he is the main connection to Mussalah's empire. Ancol Port was not a nice place although the beach was popular during daytime, but I would be visiting on a night, I thought.

I responded to Gus with,

"Brilliant big man, you have just confirmed that the snake and Naylor are sleeping partners, I had met my MI6 contact who told me that Naylor was a ghost but also had his prints all over Mussalah and his empire. I think the reason he is a ghost is he is associated with the Government plus other Jakarta elitists so keeps himself out of the spotlight leaving his partner, a certain Liam Harper to wade in the gutter with the snake."

"Okay you mad Geordie Bastard, it sounds like you have your hands full so don't go doing anything fucking stupid without letting me know!" was Gus's reply and I knew he was eager to be part of my plan. I needed him to get more info on Mussalah &Naylor. So, I responded,

"Gus if it starts getting out of hand, you will be the first I will call, I need you on that machine to crack open the web our two slimy friends are spinning, with contacts and methods being our prime motive so we can shut them down or disrupt them" Gus was the man for this and I wanted him on that role specifically as in action he does not think like me and is like a raging bull, in fact our superior in the Regiment would call him Roger Ramjet as he destroys everything in his path.

"Okay big man take care ye fucker" he had hung up and I could tell he was upset as he has never told me to take care!

I needed to visit Kathy's family today with the hope of finding her with them. That was my main aim of the day as I primarily worked for Roy. Thinking about Roy I was running low on cash, so I needed to call him for a transfer of funds. When I called, he sounded excited and asked if I had found her yet, I told him I was visiting her family today so will keep him informed of all events. I heard the desperation and disappointment in is voice as he said thanks for keeping me informed, James. I immediately thought about Putri and how much she had affected my feelings and emotion. If I never saw her again, I would be devastated and heartbroken just like Roy is now. My heart bled for the guy, and I really hoped I would find her sitting at home with her family, but alas life isn't that simple and miracles don't happen I thought. I showered and thought about Putri again which made James junior stretch into action, hopefully tonight my friend I said to myself.

I needed to get to Rawa Malang which is where the Cuzon family lived. Another area that has been neglected by the government and it was rife with criminals and prostitution. What was their life like in the Philippines to choose that area I pondered? I got the reception to order me a cab and after giving the driver the location we set off into the Jakarta traffic. It was going to be a long journey to the Cuzon family home so I spent my time daydreaming about Putri while viewing the magnificent skyline of Jakarta. After nearly 2 hours of waiting in traffic jams we had arrived and I looked at the family home. It was made of wood with a roof of different sizes of corrugated iron and plastic. It was painted a sickly color of yellow that on reflection looked like someone had vomited all over the house. There was a gate hanging on one nail to a garden that was growing vegetables and spices. I was dreading going inside and wondered if I needed inoculations to enter. A small old woman had opened the front door as I walked towards it, she had a tanned wrinkled face with white hair and I could see the faint appearance of liver spots on her face.

"Mrs. Cuzon I presume, my name is James" I said by way of an introduction, she just stood and stared at me blankly. Then a young lady appeared behind her who was a carbon copy of Kathy but a younger version, she said,

"Can I help you, my mother does not speak English and who are you, what do you want?" Charming I thought, nice greeting. The young lady in question was about 20 yrs. old, long black hair, very pretty and carrying a few pounds too much. I told her who I was and that I worked for Kathy's husband Roy from England who had hired me to find her. Her name was Yuni, she invited me in and she said that they had not heard from her sister in months. The house inside was furnished lavishly, all new equipment and as it was open plan I could see the kitchen contained all the essentials like a cooker, hob and fridge. The walls and ceilings however needed work as there was holes and damp evident in some places, but I recognized that Kathy's money was being thoughtfully spent. Yuni explained that Kathy would send money every week for her family to survive as their father had passed away many years ago and left the family penniless. Yuni said Kathy was determined not to let her family rot in poverty so left home to become the chief income provider for her family. Yuni explained that Kathy told her mother she was studying chemistry in the UK but never told her she had married. However, she had told Yuni, and said she was extremely happy with Roy whom she loved and whom looked after her. Kathy would send vast sums of money home and Yuni thought it was from her salary in England. Kathy would call Yuni at least twice a month but had stopped calling months ago, so Yuni was worried but could not call the police as she was aware that Kathy had been working as a prostitute to earn money for her new adventure in England. Kathy had told Yuni that she had found herself 2 jobs and enrolled into a college to study Chemistry as she had ambitions to be a Pharmacist here in Jakarta.

"So was it Kathy's intention to return to Jakarta after she had graduated?" I asked Yuni.

"Yes it was her plan but then she met Roy and told me that her plan was to now spend the rest of her life with Roy, but still provide for her family by sending money to us, I am really getting nervous now as you have come here to look for my sister which means she is not in England anymore"… Yuni said her voice cracking mid-sentence.

"All I can tell you is Kathy is missing and I am trying to find her, I came here in the hope she had come home but that is now obvious she didn't, however there is no indication she has come to any harm so please don't stress" I replied and reached out to grab her hand. She was shaking and I could see her eyes glazing over, I told her to not worry as I was sure Kathy would appear soon. In reality I thought Kathy was involved with Mussalah but I didn't know in what capacity. I was determined to find her however, for Roy's sanity and now her family's sake. Yuni's mother saw Yuni wiping away tears and started to cry herself, shit I don't need this. I asked Yuni to calm down and reassure her mother everything was fine then asked Yuni,

"You mentioned Kathy worked as a prostitute was that alone and do you know where?" Yuni had composed herself and responded,

"She went to a bar called Top Gun with her friend Paula and told me they had been given work in that bar serving punters and extras I suppose as she was making lots of money" I bet she was, but not as a whore I thought.

"Did Kathy mention ever going away for periods?" I asked Yuni,

"No it was only when she was leaving for the UK when she told us she was going away but she regularly flew to Singapore and back with punters she told us" very interesting I thought as they must be test flights for her mule duties making sure the bags don't burst inside her.

"One last thing, where is Paula?" I asked

"Paula is still working at the bar as far as I am aware as I called her after my sister had not called me, she said Kathy was still in the UK but will be returning soon" I needed to speak to Paula was my immediate thought.

"Can I have yours and Paula's number please?" I asked

"Sure" Yuni replied.

"I need to go as I have a special date tonight, but now I have your number I will contact you when I find Kathy, please stay calm and remember I am a phone call away if you need me, it's been a pleasure to meet you and your mother but I must go" I tried to reassure Yuni as best I could but I feared Kathy was part of Mussalah's murky trade. I also needed another shower after sitting in the Cuzon house with no AC. I was drenched with sweat so told the taxi driver to turn his AC to max when getting in his car.

While travelling back to my hotel I thought a lot about what Yuni had told me about her sister. I felt a rage in my stomach that scumbags had taken advantage of a young lady who was trying to keep her family alive. I thought about Mussalah and the many ways I wanted to kill him which started me shaking with anger. This piece of shit is funding the very people who should be administering justice to him. The whole situation is a mess but it's not exclusive to Indonesia as this happens in many countries. I needed to calm down and relax so I forced myself to think about Putri and hopefully having a special night with her resulting in a wonderful climax. Now she was in my mind I became at peace and hoped she was the girl that would change my life forever. We had arrived at my hotel which incidentally would be the last time as I planned on moving tomorrow. I scanned the area as I went inside but saw no danger or anything suspicious then went upstairs to make myself respectable for the evening with Miss Delishus. I chose Loewy's as it has many exits plus it is a driveway away from the main road, so whoever drove up to the restaurant I would be able to see them, also it is well established as a popular expat eatery, with many office folk and high rollers attending, so anything suspicious would stick out like a sore thumb. I arrived early as planned to surveil the joint and get a table with the wall behind me viewing who was coming in and leaving. I saw nothing untoward just people enjoying themselves and eating good food. I relaxed and waited for Putri. She arrived getting out of a Cab wearing a white trouser suit that was strapless and highlighted her fantastic body, her hair was left flowing down her back and she walked with pride. As she entered she saw me and waved then walked towards me, with every male head turning to look at her leaving their own dates fuming with them.

I could not get over how beautiful she was and how lucky I was, she sat opposite me with a smile that lit up the whole room and melted my heart. I ordered a bottle of wine, then we both ordered food talking as if we had known each other for years. She was mesmerizing, captivating and all mine. At the end of the meal I suggested that I would like her to come back with me and stay the night, she agreed with a smile and knowing look in her eye. I wanted to wrap her up in cotton wool and carry her to some exotic island, but had to keep her safe first so I suggested we walk to my hotel, which she shook her head at and said let's get a Grab car. These are private cars with their owner drivers who try to make a living picking up passengers to their destination. Like a taxi, but cheaper. It was not part of my plan but I agreed. However when the Grab arrived I pretended to drop something inside the car so I was out of view from prying eyes, Putri thought this was hilarious and told me to sit up and we will find what you dropped when we stop. As we had vacated the restaurant vicinity, I announced I had found my phone which resulted in a gasp of relief from Putri.

On the way to my room I asked her if she likes rum, and she said yes but not much as she didn't drink a lot. What a girl I thought a rum drinker like me. When in the room I poured her some Old Monk and coke which she described as the best tasting drink she had ever had. I love her was my immediate thought.

We drank some more and talked until she suggested that she needed a shower, this was my chance,

"Let's shower together" I said

"Good idea" she replied with a sexy smile. From that moment onwards I was in heaven, James Jnr stayed strong for a record time and I had never experienced love making like with Putri before. She was sexy, athletic, very flexible and very confident in her body and actions. I thought she had been carved from porcelain as her skin was blemish free and so smooth, she amazed me and took my breath away. I was definitely in love and it felt so good. I even at one point announced that I loved her which she replied "I love you to Alan".

Shit I had to tell her who I was and my reason for being in Indonesia. So when we finally stopped having sex I told her everything, my name, I was looking for Kathy and working for British Intelligence, plus Mussalah. She looked very concerned but said

"Please always come back to me honey, promise!"

"Always and I will always look after you" was my response, which I meant. I would love and protect this girl until I die I thought. I told her my plans which involved going to Top Gun bar and seeing Mussalah, I also told her I was leaving this hotel and moving to Grand Kemang in Kemang. However, I said the next time I meet you will be in another hotel which I will let you know when I move to it, this was to keep her safe and not to start looking for me in an area that Mussalah and his goons would be plying their trade.

"James, please stay safe and be careful" was her response

"I intend to my dear, I will be in touch with you very soon" I said, then we showered and dressed for breakfast. While eating breakfast I felt my stomach knot as this could be the last time I see Putri. I looked at her and she must have sensed my thoughts as she started crying saying she didn't want to leave me I felt the same way but needed to focus on my job, so I comforted her, telling her she would never ever be leaving me and that my heart will be inside of her forever cuddling her heart. This is what love feels like, ecstasy, heartbreak and concern it felt good.

When it was time for her to leave I felt empty as I watched her making her way to her Grab, she was crying and never stopped looking back at me. This is when I thought about Roy and the last time he had watched Kathy go, what would he have done if he knew he would never see her again? I felt like running after Putri and just saying 'fuck it, let's run off together'. I knew I couldn't do that, but I needed to protect her and keep her safe and I knew the man for that job. I went back to my room and called Gus straight away.

"Hello, who is this?" in a rough Scottish accent

"James, I need you here to do a job for me" I responded

"About fucking time, who needs to die?"

"No one I hope, I want you to protect someone for me,"

"I am on my way, send me the details of where you are and I will be there pronto" said Gus. He was a true friend never asking who needed protecting, but knew if I was asking they were important. I sent him my new hotel details and that I would be waiting in the bar for him. Gus will already be prepared as it's our way to be ready for a call for help. I went to Kemang by Grab which automatically made me think about Putri and smile. I checked in the hotel and made my way to the bar awaiting the big man. He of course knew the area and hotel as we would situate ourselves here on operations many years ago. I heard him coming before I seen him as I could hear the Flower of Scotland being sung by the crazy bastard. He saw me and shouted

"Buaidh no Bas!" In his Scottish twang which means victory or death, so I replied

"Alba gu brath" meaning Scotland forever. He laughed and said,

"I fucking love you Fraze" Gus never hid behind any false persona, he was a raw, rough, pure bred Scotch man who would die for me if I asked him to. I ordered him a beer then told him all about Putri and that I wanted him to shadow her wherever she went watching for anything suspicious or anyone watching her.

"You fucking mad Geordie, have you fell in love, you silly fucker?" was his response, then

"She must be special to do all this, so if I find any Fuckers watching her can I exterminate them?"

"Yes to the first question and if you can dispose of them cleanly, do as you want with the bastards" I replied

"I knew this day was going to be a good day, understood loud and clear, when do I meet the lucky or unlucky lady then Fraze?"

"You don't, you keep your distance and incognito, I don't want her spooked or always looking for you, I want her to carry on as normal not knowing she has a raving lunatic looking after her. I will show you her and where she lives from a distance then it's down to you to keep her safe"

"Sounds like a plan, when you planning on meeting old snake hips?" was his response and I knew he was thinking that Mussalah would act quickly after knowing I was on his trail, so watching Putri would begin asap.

"I have no intention of meeting the Snake as if I am in his space I would kill the bastard, so I am gathering intelligence on him and his dealings while I find Kathy. My guess is Snaky knows where she is so I need that info, its how I get it is the problem for now, but I will work it out" I said to Gus.

"Don't go killing him without me Fraze, I would love to skin the greasy bastard alive!"

"You and me both big man, right I need to take you to Putri's apartment and for you to recognize her. We will watch from a distance" We got a grab to her apartment block in Setiabudi. We went to a local warung and waited hoping she would be either coming out or going in to the block. I had mixed feelings about this as I had put this beautiful lady into danger but I was in love with her, and didn't want to lose her, so the best man to protect her for now was sitting right next to me. We were in luck as she came out of the building wearing tight lycra with headphones, so she must be going for a run or doing exercise.

"That's her Gus" I said

"Get the fuck out of it Fraze, she is fucking gorgeous are you sure?"

"Yes that's Putri and yes she is"

"I can honestly see the attraction, Fraze, but what does she see in you?" he laughed

"You cheeky twat, I am a highly sought after catch and she is the lucky one that caught me!" I declared

"Fraze, I will guard her with my life, but promise me if she has a sister introduce me to her" I laughed and said

"Deal, just take care of her for me mate" I almost pleaded, but knew Gus would be her guardian angel and keep her safe.

"Right he said, I need a car and a gun so I am off to see an old friend"

"I will come with you as I need a gun also" we then left but I knew Gus would be back very soon and I needed to get ready for the Star wars Café later on.

Gus gave me a lift back to my hotel in his new car, I had a Glock stuffed in my jeans and I needed to ready myself for later. I bid farewell to Gus telling him I would contact him in the morning and he said 'aye' and sped off to do his duty. I called Charlie telling him about my plan to visit Top Gun and my visit to Kathy's family. He asked if I needed him and I said no as I don't want to make things easy for Mussalah and his cronies. Its best I am alone at this stage as I will just look like a tourist looking for fun I told him, then told him I will update him of all events tomorrow and arranged a meet at the Irish Bar Murphy's in Kemang around 10am. He said perfect I will have some breakfast while you fill me in about Mussalah. I hid my gun in my room but strapped my knife to my ankle in case it was needed then I headed out to Blok M. It was a good half hour walk from tourist heaven to degradation land. The whole city seemed to change as it became darker with sprawling disgusting apartments on both sides of the road towards Top Gun. People were hanging from balcony's shouting and spitting, women were screaming, kids were screaming and I was being abused in Bahasa. Welcome to hell I thought. I approached the bar noticing a group of not very well dressed women outside smoking and on seeing me they all shouted

"Hey mister do you want a fuck?" not a trick question as the simple answer was No!!

I pushed past this coven of witches and entered the den of inequity. As I walked in 2 men were stood either side of the door and both were well built, with buzz haircuts and certainly not bouncers. I said hello to the one on my right and kept walking towards the bar. The place was full of whores and men. In the middle of the joint was a pool table with whores competing against idiot men for money. The whores were going to win after hours of practice, in fact they were competition standard. I got to the bar after fighting off lots of approaches by hungry whores asking if I wanted to party with them. I kept smiling saying I need a beer first. I got my beer but felt exposed at the bar so made my way to a chair with a wall behind me and a better view of the clientele. As I sat down I took a brief look around, there was a band playing in the upper corner watched by lots of punters and there he was Mussalah with his guests. He looked like someone had poured oil over him and every time he spoke his tongue would dart out of his mouth as if looking for flies to catch.

Next to him was a skinny man with a large nose like a pelican who had 2 ladies next to him. They were both well-toned and dressed all in black but one had long jet black hair and the other had long blond hair with both wearing it in a ponytail. They looked and acted like well-trained bodyguards as they watched everyone around them. Also on Mussalahs table was a small ugly bald man who had a facial twitch, he reminded me of Uncle Fester. He was sat with a small local girl who looked like her head had been squashed. I kept scanning the place but had a sense I was being watched but could not see anyone watching me. I was then approached by a whore wearing a very tight fitting dress, she was tiny, slim, pretty with black hair and she grabbed my leg and said

"Hello handsome do you want to fuck me tonight? You can fuck my pussy my ass or I can suck your dick!" Charming I thought what a lovely girl,

"Maybe later I just want to listen to the band and have a drink first, what's your name?" I said,

"Bercinta saya" she said

"Nice name, does it mean anything in English?" I asked

"Yes it means fuck me"

"Wow I bet you were popular at school" I responded, which she laughed and said,

"I gave the best blow jobs at school, I was very popular"

"You must have made your parents so proud, look can I see you later as I really need a drink," I said

"Okay, I will find you" she proclaimed. I hope not I thought disgusting little slut.

As she walked away I had never saw that pelican nose had walked up to me with Ting and Tong in tow. He said,

"Hi I am Liam and I own this fabulous joint and you are new here as I never forget a face" So this is Harper I thought and said,

"Hi Liam, Alan and its someplace I fully agree who are the 2 ladies" I asked,

"Oh these 2 lovelies are my fuck buddies and are very good" he said putting his arms around them and grabbing their breasts while they had both moved their hands to his groin area smiling. I thought he was a sexual predator devoid of all morals and his 2 buddies were more than sex partners as I could tell Ting and Tong were highly trained operators. I wondered why he had approached me as I was looking like a normal punter, was I getting sloppy, so I asked

"Is there a problem as I just came in to watch the band and maybe have some fun later"

"No not at all I saw you were new and wanted to introduce myself and maybe help you find a nice lady, but I see you had met one of my girls so have a good night" then he walked away, but Tong (black hair) kept staring at me so I winked at her which made her eyebrows rise while stepping towards me, I readied myself but she had second thoughts and turned after her master. Well that turned out well I thought then noticed Fester was walking towards me with the munchkin in tow. Jesus I am popular tonight. Fester walked straight up to me offering his hand saying

"I am Daz, you are new so if you want a girl my friend here will arrange one for you" every time he spoke his face twitched and I wanted to just put my fist through his face. His munchkin then spoke,

"I am Dewi and I can get you what you want for a good price, Daz likes them young don't you," which he got excited by. I really wanted to kill these degenerates here and now but said,

"That would be brilliant, I have a particular fondness for Phillipino girls so if you could supply me with one of those I would be very grateful" Munchkin said no problem How young? I told her she needed to be legal, so she gave me her number and asked me to give her a missed call so she had my number. All the time this was going on I noticed Mussalah looking across at me and Fester getting excited. I needed to get out of here and shower to rid myself of the disgusting smell that had landed on my skin. I decided to leave as I had all I needed but could not identify Kathy or indeed Paula. I finished my drink and walked out.

On exiting that shit hole I walked towards the end of the road and while walking I heard a car slowing down behind me, was I followed I thought and I have no gun, shit keep walking but at a normal pace. The car caught up to me and the front window came down with the driver in an American accent saying

"Get in the back"

"Fuck off" I replied, then a another American voice from the back seat said

"Please get in the car now as you are being watched on camera, don't look in the back just get in as if you have ordered this car" This was against everything I had been trained to do but he had said please which if anyone is going to kill you do not do, so I opened the door and got in sitting next to a man with short white/grey hair but he wasn't old enough to have complete grey hair, so he obviously dyed it. He looked at me and said

"I am Agent Mathers of the American Intelligence Agency and the man driving is Agent Trump, please hear me out before you decide to get out but we will be driving while I tell you this" I stayed quiet and let him speak,

"We have been staking that joint out for nearly a year now and with you walking in has caused panic amongst my team and no doubt Mussalah and his crew"

"I don't understand, I just went in for a drink and some fun" I finally spoke. Pleading innocence,

"I recognized you as soon as you walked in my friend" friend, I am not your friend and what does he mean recognized me? I thought

"You have the wrong man I am afraid, I have never met you in my life and just a word of advice if President Trump does not stop the car soon I will kill you both!"

"That I have no doubts you can do, but hear me out as you will find what I will say very interesting, if you don't then you can kill us" Mathers said

"Okay but make it quick!" I replied

"A few years ago we had infiltrated Jose Cordoba's organization, you will be aware that he is the biggest drugs cartel in Columbia, then one day in a bar in Medillin my agent was part of a group of Cordoba's men with his right hand man Pablo Sanchez when he watched Sanchez who was a maniac be killed by a man who he described as fearless, sharp and very fast. You will remember Sanchez as he had a scar from cheek to cheek" that bastard I thought, the one I had embedded my knife into his throat, very interesting, so I said,

"Carry on, I am all ears"

"Well my agent photographed this killing machine sending the photo to me and the agency before destroying the phone" Shit, very sloppy on my behalf, I thought, then said

"Who else did he give the photo to?"

"Just my boss" intervened agent Trump

"I had never seen someone react so fast and skillfully to take down one of the most feared man in all of Columbia, I took the photo of you secretly without being seen and left when lots of guns were pointed at us, I thought you were some sort of agent but only told my superiors. I was happy to see Sanchez dead as he was unpredictable so when questioned by Cordoba I said nothing" said Trump

"Okay so how are you now sitting in front of me as no one got out of that cartel alive" I responded

"Exactly sir, I am a dead man" to which Mathers interrupted and said

"Because his main man was executed Cordoba went crazy purging the bar he died in and ordering all his men that were there to see the demise of Sanchez to be shot and hanged in public for shaming him, we had to get Trump out pronto so we organized a raid killing all the perps including Trump, however we only killed Trump here with rubber bullets, which is why he is sat there. Our operation was compromised because of your actions so we pulled out. Agent Trump however, had gleaned a considerable amount of information on Cordoba's trade which includes his trade with Mussalah, but we are not here for him we are here for the main protagonist Steve Naylor. He is the puppet master with ties to many government figures not just herein Indonesia but Western countries like Russia and Italy. We need him on a platter so we can take his empire down the problem we have is no one has seen Naylor for over 20 yrs. so we do not know what he looks like. His parasitic partner Harper is his front and he uses Mussalah to deflect attention from him and his legitimate shipping business."

"Very convenient, so he ships drugs through his 'legitimate' business and advertises it with N & H Shipping on every shipment, like hiding in plain sight" I responded

"Naylor has many esteemed contacts as he seems to mix in the upper society circles, all we know about him is he is English and educated at Oxford, so he has influential friends"

"Well that figures as only the upper class, Conservative MP's, terrorists and gangsters are educated at Oxford" I responded

"So Agent Mathers, what are you wanting from me?" I asked

"Call me Clifton and that's Donny driving"

"Really! Donny fucking Trump, now this feels dodgy" I exclaimed

"It's really Donald but I call myself Donny as I hate that bastard who is president" announced Trump

"We don't want anything from you"...... "James... James Fraser" I replied

"Fraser the eraser very apt" was Clifton's response,

"No just Fraze will do!" I snapped back,

"Okay James, as I said we don't want nothing from you, but when you walked in that bar alarm bells started ringing in my head as I recognized you immediately and I thought you were there for one thing and that's to kill someone, but we can't let that happen this time as we know something big is happening and we can't have you fuck it all up this time. Also you attracted a lot of attention from the deviants which tells us they are getting nervous and checking everyone who enters that disgusting place, so what are you here for James?" enquired Clifton,

"Nothing that you think Clifton, I am a P.I. looking for a missing Phillipino woman who was used as a drug mule by Mussalah. I thought she would be in there but I never saw her. She has a friend called Paula who works in there so I was hoping to find her also. I gave my number to that little ugly munchkin as she claimed she would get me a Phillipino girl, I really wanted to snap her fucking neck to be honest. The other reason I was there is because British Intelligence hired me to disrupt Mussalahs business so I was there to also remind myself about the Ular" I told Clifton who looked at me with deep suspicion, then said,

"Right eraser, a few things you left that shithole without a lady which will arouse suspicion amongst Mussalah and Harper so you need to go back and find a girl, I am going back and I will ask around for Paula as I am known to punters and the management so I won't arouse any suspicion. Watch were I sit and when I have found her I will leave my glass half full and be gone, so don't overstay your welcome. The other thing is you can't disrupt Mussalahs operations as that will make Naylor go further underground and out of our reach. I will speak to my superior to relay this to London and keep you out of our way. One last thing, do not go back in the bar without a good excuse for leaving, buy some condoms and if asked say you had forgot yours and needed them to fuck the ladies from there. Right Donny stop at the nearest Alpha and then take us back to hell" Clifton explained, I liked him as he was upfront efficient and clever. When I was in the Alpha I bought condoms and sedatives as after taking one of those girls back I had no intention of fucking it even with a condom on. I just hoped Clifton could find Paula, but I thought Stella would have a heart attack when the yanks called her, which made me smile.

We got back to the bar and I saw the cameras outside this time, the plan was for me to go in alone after getting out of the car with Clifton arriving about 20mins later. As I got out Clifton said,

"I will see you soon eraser" fucking Yankee idiot I thought. I entered into the bar to a crowd of ladies surrounding me shouting the same stupid things as before. I kept walking as I seen the little whore who propositioned me previously, I approached her and said

"Did you miss me Bercinta?" she laughed and said

"I did wonder where you had gone, call me Cha Cha"

"Okay Cha Cha, I need a drink then me and you are going to party"

"That sounds like fun you have made me very horny" Cha Cha announced. I had scanned the bar while she spoke and noticed Snaky had not moved. I also saw Fester was now seated near Snaky but Harper was walking about like King Dick with Ting and Tong in tow. Cha Cha had moved a chair next to mine and was stroking my leg while looking at me and licking her lips.

"My, you are very eager" I said,

"I want your cock" she proclaimed, and I thought, well you are going to be very unlucky cos its mine and I am keeping it for someone very special. Cha Cha was really good at her job as she was getting closer to James Jnr and making him wake from his slumber. This had to stop, so I said

"Cha Cha can we wait till we are somewhere more private… please?" she looked at me all disappointed and said

"I will fuck with everyone watching me I like that"

"I don't so let's wait!"! I replied. Then all of a sudden Harper was in my space, I wanted to rip his throat out as I looked at him, but he spoke saying,

"You have returned, I thought you had left us"

"No, I left my condoms in my hotel so popped out to the Alpha to buy some new ones. As the Lone Ranger said to Tonto, never ride bareback, always saddle up my red faced friend" I responded to Harper, which he found hilarious saying,

"I like that, I will use that myself, and it looks like you have your ride for the night Mr. Ranger, little Cha Cha here will use all your condoms up as she takes some satisfying… Don't You Cha Cha?" as he spoke he grabbed her groin region, and Cha Cha smiled uncomfortably, he was a dangerous disgusting sexual predator and I wanted to end his life, Ting and Tong were behind him stroking each other and laughing. What a fucking trio I thought. I had also seen Clifton walk in and sit down as Harper spoke. I needed to get out of here fast so hopefully Clifton finds Paula soon. As I was thinking this I saw Clifton leaving so I looked at where he was sitting and saw his glass half empty. I looked at him leaving and he was followed by a lady. He found her what a guy I thought again.

"Right loose pants it's time to go and party" I said to Cha Cha loudly so Harper could hear,

"At last I think my pussy was about to close up" she replied. What a lovely girl she is.

"I think you are perfect marrying material, young lady" I joked,

"I am already married and he has a small dick" was her reply,

"So, very happy together then" I said,

"No" she replied,

"It wasn't a question to be answered Cha Cha I was being sarcastic"

"Oh right...but I am not happy with him as he..."

"Enough please I can guess the rest, I am going to make you very happy Cha Cha"

"I hope so as I love sucking cock" came her reply, which made me stop talking as I had heard enough. We left together and when outside she said to me that her price would be high as she was staying the night with me as the usual punters just get a quick 20 mins in one of these flats that we all use. Jesus the fucking degradation and diseases these people are carrying must be unknown to the World Health Organization. I scanned the area for Clifton and Trump but they were gone so tomorrow we would meet again, I thought.

"Where are we going?" Cha Cha said

"The Grand Kemang" I replied

"Very nice, let's get a taxi" so we got in a taxi and went back to my room. I had zero intention of having sex of any kind with Cha Cha which is why I bought the sedatives. When in the room she ran straight for the bed jumped on it and started to remove her clothes, I told her to get in when she was undressed while I make us both a drink. When I made her drink I put a lot of sedatives in which was enough to knock out a horse or keep her asleep for some time. She would awaken wondering if she had sex so I would spread some condoms on the floor and I would be vacating this hotel the next morning. Cha Cha will have the best sleep of her life. I went into the bedroom and she was lying on top of the bed naked with her legs wide open and she said,

"It's time to park your submarine". To which I replied,

"Drink first and you need to shower"

"Okay, will you shower with me?"

"Yes, but drink up first" She went out in seconds after glugging the drink down in one. I was relieved that it worked. I picked her up and put her in the bed she was very light, had a nice body but God knows what she was infected by.

I sat in the armchair watching her sleep in her tranquilized state and thought about Putri. I dosed off thinking about her smile and her love for me. My phone ringing woke me out of my slumber. It was Clifton and I looked at my watch I had been asleep for hours with the daylight beginning to appear,

"Hello Agent Mathers" I said

"Eraser, I found Paula and her address"

"Good news, Special Agent, we need to meet, Murphy's Irish Bar at 10am"

"Good choice eraser, I will be there"

I showered and dressed for the meeting while Cha Cha remained in a forced slumber. I wondered how much longer she would be out when she moved and began opening her eyes,

"You are very good Cha Cha, but I think I wore you out" I said

"You must be very fit as I can't remember much" she said eyeing the condoms spread over the floor,

"Really! I have to thank you for the best sex ever. I have just awoke myself and showered as I need to be somewhere soon, So get your sexy body out of bed, shower and get home to your husband" I responded to her. I needed her out of here but I needed her to think we had amazing sex in case she was asked by certain people.

"I really think we should fuck again so I remember how good you are!" she proclaimed. That's not the plan at all I wanted her gone and as far away from me as possible

"Unfortunately, as I really take a long time I can't, besides you have totally drained me and I really need to go very soon" I said, hoping she would get the message.

"I will pay you double Cha Cha as you were so good"

"Okay then let me shower then you can pay me" she said as she got out of the bed and approached me for a kiss. I reciprocated then gave her a gentle slap on her ass saying,

"Don't take forever please" I felt degraded but wanted her to feel a million dollars. She showered then dressed into her clothes from last night, then I paid her double plus extra for her taxi and some breakfast for herself. She thanked me, saying she hoped to meet me again so whenever I was in Top Gun again I must ask for her. I enthusiastically agreed and told her I wanted nobody but her. She then left feeling very proud of herself and as she went out the door I hoped she would be okay, then I thought, she has survived long enough doing what she does so she will survive even longer.

I broke out of my thoughts decided to wait about 20 mins so Cha Cha was gone then headed to Murphys. I entered the bar which was nearly empty aside from Charlie tucking in to a full Irish breakfast on his own. I walked to him and sat down with Charlie declaring that I must have the breakfast as it was delicious. I declined ordering a bacon and egg bun with a black coffee. While waiting for my order I told Charlie about everything that had happened last night. I also told him that we would be dining with the CIA very soon, which made him lift up from his food and look surprised. He said,

"I don't think we should be working with the Americans and Miss Mathews will be pissed" good I thought, Stella having a seizure would be fine by me, but I replied,

"What's wrong with working with the Yanks? They are our allies Charlie"

"Yes I agree, but they tend to keep information to themselves and leave us carrying the carnage they cause" said Charlie. Well if that's all the problems they cause it wouldn't bother me as the carnage part appealed to me.

"Charlie you will like Clifton he seems a nice genuine guy, I am sure you will get on!" I replied, wondering how late he was going to be.

"Just as my order arrived Clifton entered with Agent Trump and a woman who was flanked by 2 men dressed in black suits wearing sunglasses. 'Really' I thought who the fuck is this with the Men in Black. Clifton said hi and offered his chair to the lady, she was in her fifties, average height, slim and dressed conservatively. Clifton pulled up a chair exclaiming,

"This is Chief Targeting Analyst for the Asian Continent Thelma Page and she wants to speak to you James. You have met Donny and the other guys are Ms. Page's security detail."

"Well that's a mouthful, we used to say this my boss in the good old days, Pleasure to meet you Thelma, this is Charlie Mcall of MI6" I responded I watched Page as I spoke and noticed her surprise as I called her by her first name, she seemed a bit uptight. Clifton spoke again,

"I found your Paula, I spoke to her and she doesn't know where Kathy is"

"That's nice special agent but I never asked you to speak to her just find her as I will be talking to her!" I said in an angry response and noticed Charlie's eyebrows rise.

"Take it easy Eraser, I just asked her were her friend Kathy was, I also told her you wanted to meet her so could we have your address and phone number which she gave me, I have written it down and it's all yours" Clifton said as he pushed the paper to me.

"Okay sorry maybe I reacted badly but this case is important to me and thanks Cliffy" was my response which made Clifton sit back and relax. Then Thelma spoke,

"Mr. Fraser my special agent thinks very highly about you and only wants to help you in your quest to find your subject, however, it has come to my attention that you could jeopardize our operation searching for your subject, an operation we have been pursuing for a long time at a considerable cost so we need you to step back"

"Well Thelma, my subject is a person and I have no intention of ruining your operation! So you can fuck off!" I replied with maybe too much rage.

"James calm down and apologize to Miss. Page" said a flustered Charlie. I was taken aback by his bravado,

"Charlie I only apologize for my use of words, but this lady is not my employer so therefore does not get to tell me what to do!" I replied,

"You have mistaken my meaning Mr. Fraser, I no way wanted to offend you or tell you what to do in fact I was going to offer you some work!" Thelma had jumped in and uttered,

"I already have 2 employers and don't want anymore, besides I don't work for Yanks" I announced but wondered what she had in mind, which she will no doubt tell me soon but then Charlie jumped in again,

"I am sorry Miss Page but James works for British Intelligence so cannot be employed by yourselves" nice one Charlie boy! I thought. Then Clifton spoke,

"James we will be putting immense pressure on your government and MI6 to make you step away from our op. But we want you to execute Mussalah for us!"

"Well that changes things Special agent, but wouldn't killing the Snake fuck up your op?" I said with interest, Thelma jumped in,

"No it will help us, as Naylor would have to be more prominent and he is our prime target. With Mussalah, he has many enemies so an assassination of him would not result in the local authorities looking to far afield if you get my meaning, we feel you are our best chance of ridding this earth of Mussalah because we know you won't fail!"

"I am sure you have people like me in America that could do this job so are you going to hang the brits out to dry over this, am I now dispensable?" I replied,

"Mr. Fraser who do you think we are? We are not assassins and certainly we do not kill one of own! You are our closest allies and our special relationship must remain, we have people in the BIN who will help tidy up the mess you will make and point the blame into another direction and we also need to be totally oblivious to this assassination as we have people entrenched within this government who will never know about this event. Yes we could send our agents like Clifton to do our dirty work but we cannot hide the fact that they are American and risk being pariahs to our allies or giving our enemies a reason to attack us, so you are our finest solution. You will also be well paid into an untraceable offshore account so no finger pointing!" Responded Thelma.

"As I was once informed 'always follow the money', so Thelma you better not advertise were my money comes from, as I can imagine you wanting to use me for many other special operations. And let me add that if I get even a sniff of a double cross you and your people need to have a very good hiding place" I proclaimed, and watched

Thelma's face. She seemed very efficient and thorough and she never made any facial movements or eye movements to indicate she was lying, but then again she is well trained. However, I trusted her. She then responded,

"Mr. Fraser I can assure you that your money will come from an unnamed account that has no connection to our agency, and you have my undying word that I am not in the business of double crossing our agents, home based or foreign, Yes you will be valuable to us as you are for your own Intelligence service but let me tell you this we will deny knowledge of ever knowing you, which I hope is how you will accept our terms!"

"Okay Thelma, You have many hurdles to overcome, one is to persuade my employers that I work for both of you as a ghost, which I agree is how I prefer to work and another hurdle to clear is I won't work alone so whatever you were paying me has just increased three-fold. I can also assure you that my men will be discrete, tenacious and as efficient as I am" I replied. I watched Clifton push out his cheeks when I finished but then he winked at me with assurance.

"Sounds like we have a deal, Mr. Fraser, welcome aboard" said Thelma and offered me her hand to shake. I was fine by these contracts as they paid well, there was no paper trail, I was my own boss and I was not linked to any organization, plus I could kill bad people without remorse. I liked Thelma and yes I trusted her word, but I knew this deal would put me in front of dangerous people who would want my head on a stake. She also had to meet frosty pants Stella who will deny all access to me and be absolutely pissed by being gazumped by the Yanks. So all things good with me. Thelma spoke again,

"Your contact will be special agent Mathers at all times. You are acquainted so everything will go through him. As for myself, I was never here and I have never met you, however, I will be speaking to your superiors very soon."

"No problem Amber, but they aren't my superiors as I am a ghost to them also so enjoy your meeting with Miss. Mathews as she is a real hottie!" I replied smiling, Then Clifton spoke,

"Eraser, we need to speak when Ms. Page has departed" No problem I thought but enough of the stupid eraser! Then Thelma Page got up and left with MIB in close pursuit. She didn't even say 'bye', which I thought was very rude of her. Clifton spoke,

"What's the plan then James?"

"My plan is to find Kathy Cuzon before I take out your mark, Mussalah, so you need to tell me where Paula lives and her number" I said

"Okay James as loyal as ever, Here are all the details on Paula, just let me know when you need me" replied Clifton as he handed me a piece of paper with an address and phone number on. The phone number did not correspond with the number Yuni gave me so maybe Paula had 2 phones or changed her number. The address was in Ciliwung pronounced Chiliwung which is a slum area of Jakarta riddled with crime, very nice I thought. Charlie then spoke,

"James, you will need to speak to Ms. Mathews before killing Mussalah"

"I am aware of that Charlie and Mussalah will stay alive until I find Kathy, so let the Yanks approach Stella first before I speak with her, okay" I replied and Charlie gave a thumbs up response. I thought about Gus and how happy he will be working for the Yanks to kill scum. I then said to Clifton,

"What's your plan my friend?" to which Clifton replied,

"We are trailing Harper to see if he can take us to Naylor, but be aware if I have anything new on Miss Cuzon I will be in touch"

"Its Mrs. Mckray Clifton and I will be much obliged" I responded to Clifton, then said

"Right gents, I think we are done here so I need to be somewhere, Clifton I will be in touch very soon and it's been a pleasure" we all left to go our separate ways, with Charlie following me. I told Charlie I needed to visit Paula but I won't be calling ahead as I want to surprise her to which Charlie said it was a good plan and a plan he doesn't need to join me on. I agreed as I thought Paula is already on the end of her nerves with working in Top Gun and having Harper and Mussalah keeping an eye on her, so to be visited by another two mysterious guests would push her over the edge. It would be best for just me to turn my charm on and reassure her when I meet her unless I turn up and Kathy answers the door. Life isn't that easy I thought so I ordered a grab and headed for Ciliwung. The night had rushed in with black clouds overhead ready for a heavy downpour when I arrived in the vicinity of Paula's apartment block. I wanted to walk to her block rather than being dropped outside, this is so I can get a feel of the surrounding area and look for any danger. As I walked to her block I had to concentrate as it was dark and the place was littered with rubbish, plastic bottles and wrecked cars. What a shit hole I thought, who the fuck would live here? As I approached Paula's block identified by a painted sign in white 'Block C 1-250' I saw something move in the shadows ahead, before I could focus I was attacked by a very quick and acrobatic entity. After a couple of front flips the black clad entity had leapt at me skimming my face with a sharp object which slashed me and drew blood. I turned towards this thing and as she landed I could see it was Tong (Black hair and Harpers fuck buddy). She had a knife which had cut me and she had crouched down ready to attack me again. Now there is a misconception about females fighting that they are weak and no match for a man, total bullshit as women are flexible, athletic, determined and they are trained to kill, just like Tong here. I needed to be calm relax and focus on her movements, Instead of attacking her I stood up straight took a deep breath and waited. She smiled and came in for the kill, she front flipped for speed then launched into a kick towards my face, with pace I caught her ankle heading towards my face with my left hand, she looked surprised so I pulled her towards me using her leg then grabbed her by the throat with my right hand and then slammed her head first to the ground where I heard her skull crack as it hit the tarmac. Her eyes closed and she went limp, she was dead and I needed to think fast as well as wait for Ting to appear. I stepped into the shadows and waited but nothing stirred, she was alone, but now I have a dead body to get rid of. I picked her up over my shoulder and carried her up the stairs of the apartment block to floor 2, I then entered the walkway which was empty luckily. I went half way along, looked over the hand rail, there was no one around 'good' I thought then threw Tong over the edge. She landed on her back below and I saw blood appear beneath her. My next thought was that Ting must have Paula, so I moved quickly to floor 3 but as I came from out of the stair well, I was met with a gun in my face then the trigger was cocked. Shit, do I have to die in this shit hole, I looked at the person about to kill me and saw it was one of the 'bouncers' from Top Gun, I waited for the bullet then saw his head explode on one side before he hit the floor. What the fuck I thought. I then heard an American voice shout,

"Eraser come here quickly," I looked around the corner and saw two figures dressed in black combats and balaclavas aiming their rifles towards me. The guy in front took of his balaclava and I recognized agent Trump. He was beckoning me over to him frantically. I obeyed and ran to him before saying'

"What the fuck is going on?" Trump replied

"Let's get out of here first then Special Agent Mathers will tell you everything" I thought I had been set up but followed Trump. We ran across the littered waste ground and entered another block of apartments to which Trump and his friend led me to the fifth floor, apartment 506, on entrance I was greeted by Clifton who told me to sit down, I didn't want to sit down as my body was trembling with rage, so I said,

"Only you and Charlie knew I was coming here so you better talk fast before I kill you all!"

"Charming, we have just saved your life and you tell us you are going to kill us, that's nice Eraser" I was ready to launch into full scale combat but instead, I said,

"Talk and no bullshit"

"I told you we were watching Harper and this is where he led us. He must be watching Paula for visitors and you walked straight into the storm!" Clifton said

"So why didn't you warn me, you know this is Paula's address?"

"Call me curious but when you arrived we waited and watched you in action, which was very impressive with the Black Widow, However you ran straight into that gun which was very sloppy, so Agent Trump and agent White went to your aid, thank you very much!" He was right I got sloppy because I wanted to save Paula, very bad James I thought. I responded with,

"So you let fucking Tong attack me knowing she was lying in wait why?"

"We did not know she was there until she attacked you, we had been concentrating on the perp on floor 3 who watched you throw her body off floor 2, you looked down but not up Eraser, so it was a good job we were here, however I like your idea of throwing the body over the top but hey don't worry about that anyway as the bozo on floor 3 has lost half his head so we will feed the BIN with an upsurge in gang violence line that they will feed the local police and press" Shit, very sloppy and I am lucky to be alive thanks to my new best friends, with the unknown agent attending to my cut from Tong, so I said,

"I apologize for my outburst and I offer my sincere thanks to all of you for saving my life, but one thing is Harper with Paula? Is Paula part of Mussalah's crew?"

"Harper is in the next apartment to Paula's, and probably watching for visitors, he went in there with a blond woman who is probably the other half of his fuck buddies, We have not seen Paula exit or enter since we arrived" said Clifton,

"So my next question is why is Harper watching Paula?"

"We don't know that answer, but can guess that he is looking for the subject that you are looking for and thinks she is going to turn up here" If Paula is not involved with Harper and Mussalah it seems logical that Kathy would surface with Paula so what the fuck has Kathy done I thought.

"I need to speak with Paula ASAP!" I said, then Trump said 'we have movement sir' as he looked through binoculars. Clifton took a look and said,

"Harper is on the move so it looks like waiting in that shit hole did not please him" I asked Clifton

"Do you think Harper is on to us?" I kept thinking why he is here.

"No, unless Paula told him about speaking to me, but I think the bigger picture is your Kathy is very important to Mussalah, with

Harper tasked to finding her!" was Clifton's response which made sense in a way, I don't think Paula would tell Harper or Mussalah anything as she would know her life would soon be ended, so maybe she is aware where Kathy is and what she has done to garner all the loving attention from all and sundry. Paula has become my number one witness in the search for Kathy. We watched Harper and Ting make their way out of the apartment block, he passed the body of the 'Bouncer' looking carefully at it then made his way out passing the body of Tong sprawled out and destroyed on the tarmac, Ting got all upset but Harper stopped her touching the body, they then got into a parked car and drove off. Clifton packed up his things and said to me 'are you coming?' Hell yes! I thought. We made our way to a 4 x4 parked out of sight, White drove and skillfully maneuvered the car to within sight of Harpers. We followed him to within distance of Top Gun and watched him enter the bar.

"Problem we have now is he is aware that he is being stalked and he will tell Mussalah" I said. I was also getting worried for Paula.

"That I can guarantee Eraser, but he doesn't know who yet. As for Mussalah, I am sure the clock is ticking for him!" responded Clifton

"Mussalah will stop breathing when I find Kathy that is a promise" I replied, I needed to speak to Gus about Putri, Charlie to let him know about what happened and Stella to receive permission to eradicate Mussalah. I spoke and said to Clifton,

"The bodies will be found soon so you need to let your inside man made aware of your plan and I need to be somewhere fast"

"The bodies will be explained with no trace to you Eraser, that I can guarantee, please don't go to Top Gun alone. We need to arrange a meeting very soon" he said. I had no intention of going to that fucking bar again, but told Clifton I would meet him in Murphy's in two days' time same time as before. As I was about to leave the car my phone rang, the number indicated it was the ugly munchkin from Top Gun.

"Hello, what can I do for you?" I said, she said that she had found me a Phillipino girl but I must go to Singapore to meet her as she was there waiting for me. Well I am not stupid enough to walk into the hands of my killer, so I told her to inform the girl to meet me in McGettigans Irish bar on Clarkes Quay at 7pm tomorrow night. A nice open place with plenty of public about so very difficult to kill me. She responded by saying she will be there but she will be with Liam Harper. I don't do threesomes I told her, to which she laughed and said Liam needed to be there to speak to me that's all. She then hung up. I relayed the full conversation to Clifton and his team who said,

"Tell me you are not going Please Eraser!" was his concerned response.

"Damn right I am going, the scumbag could be holding Kathy!"

"You are walking into a trap James!" said Clifton

"If I am then people will get hurt!" I replied

"We can't help you in Singapore James or clean up after you, I promise you though if you don't return I will kill Harper and Mussalah myself!"

"I will be back Clifton and Mussalah is all mine. We need to rearrange our meeting till when I return so I will be in touch" I bid them all farewell as I needed to be somewhere. I contacted Gus who had nothing to report which was a relief, then I contacted Charlie to meet me in the Ritz-Carlton in Kuningan, which will be my new hotel. Security is very tight in this hotel so it's a good choice plus it's where I am planning on meeting Putri again when I get back from Singapore. After clearing out and checking out of the Grand Kemang, I made my way to the Ritz-Carlton. I was checking in as Peter Beardsley, who is another of my heroes and an ex Newcastle United legend like Shearer. I informed Charlie to meet me in the bar as I needed to shower and change. I met Charlie and relayed everything that had happened and that I was going to Singapore in the morning. He looked very apprehensive saying that Ms. Mathews would need to be informed but I told him that Stella would contact me as soon as Thelma Page spoke to her. He also told me not to go to Singapore. So many people concerned about me was making me very self-conscious but humbled. I had been sloppy once but it would never happen again I thought, plus I could have done with Gus but I needed him right where he was now. I will deal with Harper and whatever he has planned but legally and discretely would be the order of the day. I was leaving for the airport early so needed to sleep and prepare. I bid farewell to Charlie and went to my room.

CHAPTER 9 CHRISTY

I boarded my flight to Singapore again from Halim and not the main International airport. I had no trouble at the check in as Peter Beardsley so all going well. I had a call from Putri before boarding asking when we could meet up again, to which I replied very soon as I have some business to attend to first. She sounded very pleased with the news and I was very happy also. On arrival at Singapore I hit a problem at immigration as the officer happened to be a Newcastle fan and recognized the name. I told him unfortunately for the ex-footballer we share the same name but we are not related, although 'I wish I was then I could ask him for free tickets to every home game', which the officer laughed and said 'it is my dream to watch Newcastle United at home, you are very lucky to be able to watch them'. 'Yes, I replied if I could afford the ticket', he laughed again and scanned me through. Newcastle fans are everywhere I thought. I had booked into my usual hotel on Orchard Road the Orchard Rendezvous which is in reality on Tanglin Road but is excellent strategically to get on Orchard Road and also disappear through nearby outlets. It is also opposite the notorious Orchard Towers. I wanted to be early so I could do some reconnaissance of the area with escape routes high on my agenda. When I had done all I needed to do, I ate at Jamie's Italian, then went back to prepare for my meeting with Pelican Beak (Harper). I had no weapon so I wanted to be at McGettigans before Harper so I could survey the area and surroundings then situate myself outside in the beer garden with lots of people walking past and with my back against a wall viewing the entrance as people arrived. I didn't expect Harper to try anything stupid but whoever he was with might be totally oblivious to their surroundings. I needed to prepare carefully and be aware of all possibilities. I arrived an hour early at the bar, I looked around and could not see Big Nose so I went inside looked around, he wasn't here yet. I went into the front beer garden found an ideal bench with the bar itself behind me and I watched for all visitors arriving. I ordered a black coffee while waiting as I wanted to be fully alert. On the stroke of 8pm, Harper and Ting got out of a black limo, then I noticed 2 large gentlemen exit from the other side of the limo, let the fun begin I thought. Harper seen me and waved, the fucking prick, he was dressed in a pin stripe suit with a red tie, white shirt and shiny shoes, he walked towards me looking around with the hope people were watching him. In fact people were watching Ting who was dressed in a black skin tight vinyl/lycra one piece outfit that she fit very nicely into. With her long blonde hair in a ponytail she looked like an Asian catwoman. I watched the 2 goons take a bench to my left facing us so I thought nothing going to happen here tonight, good, let's get started. Harper extended his hand to shake so I made a fist and said fist pump only as I don't know where that's been and looked at Ting, she wasn't amused.

"Where's the Phillipino girl or is it her?" I asked pointing to Ting

"What happened to your face?" he said

"I had too many rums and fell over" I responded

"We need to talk Mr. Shearer, why are you interested in Phillipino's?" Harper spoke,

"Probably the same reason you are interested in threesomes with Asian sisters!" I replied

"Touché but you see I only have 2 Phillipino's working for me and as it happened one has gone missing" responded Harper, interesting I thought I had read him as he spoke and he never showed any indication of lying. So who was missing? I needed to reveal some things to this scumbag first, but some fun first

"Where's the other half of Ting and Tong?" I asked

"Susie is not feeling very well so she stayed in the hotel" he said. And there it was, his tell, he moved his eyes to the left when he said that indicating he was lying,

"Oh that's unfortunate I hope she doesn't fall into something serious and she gets back on her feet very soon" I replied and noticed Ting's body go rigid as she stared her death glare at me. Harper never flinched and just smiled, then lied again by saying,

"She will be back to her normal self, real soon" his eyes moving again to the left,

"Can I ask you a question Liam as this has been bothering me since you arrived?"

"Of course, fire away"

"Can you dig for worms with that nose of yours?" I asked and watched Ting nearly explode internally, Harper however, just smiled and said,

"It's very useful to the ladies Mr. Shearer believe me" he thinks he is a comedian. He was starting to irritate me now and I wasn't getting any closer to finding Kathy, so it was time to talk business,

"I am a Private Investigator hired by Kathy Mckray's husband to find her and I believe you know where she is!" I announced, Harper looked at me in amazement and said,

"I don't know anyone called Kathy Mckray and none of my girls are married" eyes to the left again as he spoke,

"You might know her as Kathy Cuzon"

"Ahh my missing girl, I was thinking you had her!" this time no eye movement, so he doesn't know where she is,

"Look just tell me about Kathy?" I asked

"She worked in my bar to earn money for her family or some shit like that, however Andre became fond of her and recruited her to act as a drug mule. She was very good at her job, but after her last run to the UK she vanished!" he said looking directly into my eyes,

"Who the fuck is Andre?" I responded,

"Eh, oh Mr. Mussalah to you"

"The snake!" I said mimicking my tongue in and out. Harper laughed uncontrollably and nodding his head saying

"Yes, him"

"So Kathy has never returned to Jakarta since her time in the UK?" I asked

77

"Not to my knowledge as she has never returned to the place she shares with her friend and we can't locate her in the UK" was his response, again with no eye movement. What the fuck has happened to her I thought.

"She seems to be having lots of fun over in the UK as she is married according to you and she also kept one of the bags inside of her which is worth half a million dollars as our customers in Liverpool complained of being conned by Andr… Mussalah!" he spoke with no tell again and I was getting a better picture of Kathy, she just wanted to help her family and probably had enough of risking her life for the snake so she kept one bag back for herself, however after probably escaping the drug barons of Liverpool she ended up in the North East, looked for someone to marry and along came gullible Roy Mckray. She then became a legal alien of the UK with Roy's name thus hiding in plain sight from outlaws. It also explains how she was as well off as she had ripped off Asia's prime drug's baron who had also paid her a tidy sum to do his dirty work. I had total admiration for Kathy, but this did not explain where she was. I could see Harper watching me as I was putting this all together, so I said,

"I have everything I need now but one more question Why am I here in Singapore?"

"Because Mr. Shearer, I am being watched by whom I don't know yet, plus I have just escorted 2 new ladies on a test run, readying them for a client in France, of course it's safer here also for me" fucking prick I thought but he knows he is being watched so Clifton has got sloppy or he has been tipped off. I favor the last thought with secrets not being a secret if more than one person knows it, so with that bullshit, I had had enough and said,

"Thanks for your time but I need to leave"

"Going so soon Mr. Shearer and I thought we could party together" big nose declared

"I am sure Ting will be enough for your party and maybe Tong is feeling better so give her a call" I said as I got up to leave. He laughed and said

"I am sure we will meet again Mr. Shearer" A threat I presume,

"You better not hope so Pelican Beak!" I replied and walked away, but I looked back and saw Harper look at his Goons and throw his head in my direction indicating to follow me. I got in the first taxi on the rank and told him to go to the Hilton on Orchard Road. I looked back and saw the goons get in a taxi to follow me. I had planned for this earlier in the day. When I got to the Hilton I entered the lobby then headed for a side exit towards the underground entrance. I never looked back and jogged to the metro station, I waited for the passengers to disembark then I joined them to go up to Orchard Road. We all crossed to the other side with myself right in the middle of the bunch. I looked to my left and saw the 2 goons stood outside the Hilton with one of them on his phone. As I got to the other side of Orchard Road I headed back towards where the goons where. I was on the same side as the Towers or even better hopefully Christy's patch. I was in luck as I saw Christy, but she had 3 men around her, all Indians, she was arguing with them when I watched one of the men grab her arm. I walked up to them and told the one holding Christy to let her go.

"Hi Alan what happened to your face" said Christy, then the one holding her said,

"Fuck off man, she is all ours tonight!" I didn't want to make much commotion so I slammed the palm of my right hand into the bridge of his nose shattering bone and knocking him down, the other two spluttered apologies and ran away, the one on the floor was starting to scream so I quieted him down by punching him on his nose again and this time he was knocked out and quiet.

I looked across towards the goons but they had heard nothing, as the traffic was heavy and I kept the noise to a minimum, they were still stood outside of the Hilton. I looked at Christy and hugged her in a tight embrace, she then said,

"You are my hero, are we going to fuck now?" she has never changed which disappointed me.

"No Christy we are not, but you are spending the night with me and I cut myself shaving" I tried explaining, and answering her previous question

"That sounds interesting and fun, let's go then" I looked across the road and saw the goons still stood outside the Hilton, so it was time to vacate this area. I grabbed Christy's hand and walked towards the throb of people outside the Towers walking through them as cover, as soon as we cleared the crowd I walked right instead of to my hotel, I needed a seedy place to stay tonight and that's where I was heading.

"Where are we going Alan?" said Christy,

"Not far now honey" I replied.

About 5 mins later we were here, it was a 3 star hotel used by punters and girls from the towers so a perfect cover for the night. We checked in and as I had prepared my passport said Alan Shearer with his special guest Christobel???

"Sanchez" came her response showing her I.D.

"Nice name" I said

"No its not, I hate it!" there's a story there I thought but I just left it as we went to our room. I had not intended to use Christy as cover from the bad guys but now it's happened I better make the best use of things, which will disappoint Christy and even me to an extent.

"I really want to fuck you Alan!" Christy proclaimed

"To be honest with you Christy I want to with you also, but I can't, I don't look at you that way which is strange as I have feelings for you but in a best friend/close relation way, besides I am in a relationship with someone I love" I responded,

"Alan I am a prostitute, I fuck husbands, cheats, liars and scum for money. However, I don't have feelings for you but you have made me question myself since we spoke last" that sounded promising which pleased me. She was looking at me and the one double bed with a very horny look on her face. I said,

"Right I will shower first, then you can and we can get in the bed together." She looked very excited and punched the air saying,

"Yesss!!!! But why don't we shower together?"

"Christy please…its tiny in there, lets stick to the plan…okay?" she was relentless, I went to the shower while she got in the bed, I undressed in the shower and came out with the towel around my waste, she looked disappointed, She left the bed saying

"My turn so get in and wait" Jesus this is going to be a long night. I climbed in bed naked as I always sleep that way and waited for Miss. Sanchez, She emerged from the shower unsurprisingly, completely naked. She was beautiful with an amazing body, her stomach was flat and toned and her breasts were perfectly shaped, she had a smile on her face and as she saw my reaction she said,

"This is all free for you tonight you handsome man" I was flattered but forced myself to restrain my natural urges although James Junior was at full strength, Christy climbed into the bed and placed her leg over my body and said,

"My my, you are a huge guy, Mr. Shearer" she giggled, which made me laugh and relax. Christy was a survivor and she used all her street knowledge to get the best from people, I really liked her but not in a sexual way, which was not what junior was indicating. I told her I just wanted to talk and get to know her more, as the lady I have fell in love with does not deserve me being unfaithful. She disappointingly agreed to talk but said that wasn't free and I must pay. I laughed and agreed, I told her my real name and who I was and that I was looking for a missing lady and I even told her about Putri and that she had changed my whole outlook on life. Then I told her that the moment I had seen her I felt something inside of me, which was to protect you and save you from evil. She placed her head on my chest and spoke about her life, she was born in Montevideo in Uruguay to an abusive father. He would beat her mother on a regular basis then when she was 13 he raped her. For the next 3 years he would regularly creep into her room and abuse her, she hated him and his name as he was a Colonel in the local police force. Then one day she had enough so before going to her bed she went into her father's room, took his gun and waited in her bed for him to sneak in. Just as he was undressing she shot him in the chest killing him instantly, her mother ran in screaming at her telling her to get out now you little bitch you have destroyed our lives. Christy said she packed some of things and left with the gun and headed for the dock area, where she was befriended by some local prostitutes who gave her a place to stay and fed her. She also spied on them when they brought punters back. However she said all the punters seemed to be fat ugly men who stunk, so although she liked the idea of making money from sex, she did not want smelly fat men who reminded her of her father. She decided to rob the woman who befriended her and with the money she paid her way onto a container ship destined for Singapore. Again she befriended some Phillipino whores who worked at the Towers, they let her stay with them until she could afford her own place and she learnt a lot from them, plus she got a job working one of the bars in the towers. She learnt quickly in Singapore that the sexiest and most beautiful girls earn the most money so she looked after herself, cleaned herself, saw a doctor regularly, attended a gym and rented herself a small one room apartment with the money she made. She was now 27 and after I had spoken to her previously she had decided to change her life and try to enroll into college to study law. However, it's not cheap here in Singapore so she had to return to the streets to earn the money to pay for her new life. I told her I was proud of her and that I would help her, but then I heard a small grunt come from her, she was asleep on my chest and I felt so close to this young girl who had beaten adversary and her demons to try and become somebody. I wanted to protect her from evil forever. I fell asleep dreaming about Putri with Christy beside me.

I woke in the same position with Christy snoozing on my chest. I needed to get in touch with Paula ASAP as I thought she was now in danger. As I tried to move Christy stopped me from moving by clinging on to me even tighter, she asked me to stay a little bit longer as she had something else to tell me. I said okay and relaxed with my right arm still around her shoulders. She moved even more into me and started talking, she told me that when her father first started to rape her she would cry for hours after. Then she decided to become stronger and to forget what her father was doing, so she taught herself to not feel anything, to disassociate from her body and clear her mind. She said ever since she turned to being a prostitute she had performed the same act with her punters, she had become scared of never feeling emotions for anyone as she became so good at shutting out the act of sex. Whether they were on top of her or behind her she felt nothing and just used her body for the money, nothing else. However, when she had met me she felt something and she told me she had lied when she said she had no feelings for me because since the first day she met me she never stopped thinking about me and what I told her. So when I turned up last night she thought that we were going to be another Pretty Woman film.

"What" I replied, "no Christy you mean a lot to me but not in a sexual way, sorry" to which she said I understand James you have Putri and she is very lucky, but what I am trying to say is you made me have feelings that I thought had disappeared, so I will be forever grateful to you.

"You are my savior Mr. James."

"I will always be here for you Christy, but you are you are own savior and I can assure you that one day you will find your knight in shining armor and he will be the luckiest man in the world" I announced

"Christy everyone has a past but as I always say 'It's not how you start your life its how you end it' which matters the most" She grabbed me tightly and I could feel tears on my chest, she then said,

"I love you Mr. James and I will make you proud of me" I was already very proud of her, she had suffered a living hell from someone who should of protected her, but she escaped that and made something of her life albeit in the oldest profession in the world, but she had survived and was now determined to become someone. I replied

"You already make me proud Christy but I know what you mean and I have no doubt that whatever you decide to do, you will be successful, and I love you also Christobel" I kissed her forehead and hugged her tighter which made her full body relax and her head push even further into my chest. We laid like that for another hour then I told her I needed to go, she pleaded with me to stay.

"Christy I promise you that I will look after you forever, but for now I need to help someone else, please understand that my job is very dangerous and the people I help are in danger, so I need to go." She looked into my eyes and said "okay go, but I will be waiting for you" that I had no doubt she would do. I got up and dressed then I handed Christy a burner phone saying only call this number to contact me as I pointed to another burner phone. I will contact you through this method, she looked worried, so I said its fine Christy no one knows you are with me or even knows me and I aim to keep it that way. I will leave this hotel alone but I paid for 2 nights and room service so stay tonight before leaving tomorrow please.

"Okay James I will but please be safe and never forget me!"

"I will never forget you Christy and I will be in touch very soon" I kissed her forehead again and left. I needed to focus and I needed to find Paula. I also needed to contact Gus about my plan. I made my way to my hotel and saw nothing suspicious or anyone waiting outside the Hilton. When I got to my room I called Gus first, I told him about my meeting with Thelma and we had been hired to kill Mussalah,

"No way, working for the Yanks with our first mission to kill the Ular! it doesn't get any better than this" he responded. I told him about my rendezvous with Harper here in Singapore, which disappointed him as he said that's my home so why didn't you tell me about your meeting? I didn't answer but thought I needed it to be clean without a major incident we couldn't explain away, I then told him about Christy and how much this young girl had touched my life.

"You are going soft in your old age you silly fucker" was his reply. I then asked how much he took from his scammer friend, he said a lot of money, enough to buy 2 houses on Nassim Road, wow I thought nearly $3 million dollars.

"I am going to ask a huge favor my friend, can I borrow some money from you?"

"What the fuck do you mean, borrow? I will give you the money yee silly fucker, we are partners now, what do you want it for and how much?" said my Scottish friend

"It's not for me, it's for Christy to get her enrolled and through college" I told him,

"Jesus, you certainly do have a hard on for this girl and she must be worth it if you are willing to stump up for her" said Gus, yes she was I thought.

"I want you to meet her first then you will understand why, but that will be for another day, I will be telling Putri to meet me at the Ritz-Carlton in Kuningan when I return, but we need to meet to go over our plan for old Snaky!" I responded.

"Okay, I will tail her to the hotel then fuck off to let you have some fun you lucky bastard!" said Gus, I told him thanks and that I would be in touch very soon.

I then reluctantly called Paula on the number Clifton had given me. It was answered on the first ring,

"Hello?" enquired the female voice

"Is this Paula?" I asked

"Yes it is, who is calling please?" I told her my real name and that I was hired by Roy Mckray to find his wife Kathy, your friend Kathy Cuzon, and I needed to talk to her in a safe place. She responded saying she does not know where Kathy is but will talk to me, suggesting Starbucks café in Plaza Indonesia in Thamrin. Excellent I thought and told her,

"I will be there for 7pm tonight" she said she would see me there but then asked,

"How will I know who you are?"

"Good question, when I arrive I will call you with this number and if I am before you I will call every time I think it's you entering" sounds complicated but hopefully we make it work, she replied.

"See you soon Paula" I ended the call and needed to catch my flight so I ordered a taxi for the airport.

CHAPTER 10 PAULA

I had no problems at the airport this time and landed at Halim in good time to meet Putri at my new hotel then get to my meeting with Paula. When I was at Halim airport my phone rang, when I looked at the caller ID it was Stella.

"Hello Stella, what can I do for you?"

"Don't fucking patronize me James, I have just came off a 2 hour phone call with our American counterparts, a woman called Thelma Page who basically talked down to me and told me you had been hired by her!" calm down Stella, I thought,

"What can I say Stella, yes you are correct and she wants me to kill Mussalah!"

"No fucking way James, we cannot afford a diplomatic incident with Indonesia!"

Said Stella speaking to type,

"Stella don't worry the assassin will never be traced and it's for the good of all involved as it's going to lead to the identification and hopefully arrest of the real Mr. Big of Asia who only happens to be fucking English!" I responded angrily,

"I can't protect you if you go ahead with this crazy plan James" Stella said calmly,

"Stella, look at the bright side, we disrupt Mussalahs modus operandi completely, he is exterminated and we get to identify and claim responsibility for Naylor, plus you can hold your head up high knowing it wasn't us but the Yanks who assassinated Mussalah. It's a win win for you Stella." I announced

"But it's you who will be holding the smoking gun James and why where you in Singapore?" responded Stella

"Don't worry about that Stella and are you tracking me?"

"I do worry James and of course we are which you are helping by taking your phone, good idea James, and the phone I mean not the assassination!" she spluttered,

"Another thing James were you responsible for the 2 deaths in Jakarta the other day? The one that's all over the news?" she enquired.

"Don't know what you are talking about, all that's on the local news here is that there has been an increase in gang violence with 2 known gangsters killed as part of the increase. I don't get involved in local gang violence so it's nothing to do with me" I lied.

"James please take care and be careful, I hope no finger is pointed at us about Mussalah" said Stella with concern in her voice

"Stella I am touched by your concern, I think I am melting your frosty pants" I said sarcastically,

"Fuck off James!" came her reply, my, she is turning into a right fiery foul mouthed dragon, I like her even more now, I thought. I called Putri asking her to meet me at The Ritz-Carlton, telling her I would meet her in the reception in about an hour. She said she couldn't wait to see me again, which made me feel wonderful. After checking in to my room I went to meet Putri, My phone pinged and I read the message 'she is here, we will talk soon, Gus'. Brilliant I thought, as I got to the reception, she came walking through the door and I nearly fell over looking at her, she was amazing and beautiful, she ran to me, we hugged and kissed.

"I have missed you so much James" she said,

"Well lets go to our room and show me how much" I replied to which she gave a sexy giggle in response. We made love with lots of intensity and I felt elated. I then told her I had a meeting to go to later but I will be back to spend lots of time with her, which she responded with a loud cheer. I love this woman.

I got to the Starbucks in the plaza half an hour early, looked around but saw no woman sitting alone. I made my way to a seat with a clear view of the entrance and waited. Not long later a woman, very slim with long black hair entered looking flustered and scanning the café. I called Paula's number and the woman answered her phone. I said,

"I am the one waving at you!" she looked around, saw me and waved back before approaching. We exchanged pleasantries ordered some coffee then talked.

"Where is Kathy?" I said bluntly,

"I don't know, she went to the UK carrying that stuff for Mussalah and never returned" she told me

"Do you know she married?"

"Yes she called me saying she had met the most romantic and wonderful man and that she was very happy, plus she would never return to Indonesia. I said what about your family and she replied that she would send money to them on a regular basis, with the hope of getting them over to the UK with her" Interesting I thought, her love for Roy was genuine and she was never returning here, so she has never left the UK.

"Did she say anything else about living in the UK?" I asked

"She said she loved it and that it was a beautiful place to live, she said she was enrolled in a college practicing chemistry so she could become a pharmacist" I knew all this so I asked

"Was she in any trouble, like from bad men concerning the theft of the drugs?"

"Oh so you know about that. No she never mentioned anything like that but she did say that someone in her college class was paying her a lot of attention"

"Did she say who, did she describe him?"

"She said it was nothing to worry about, but he had really bad breath" well I knew who that was and it was the first time I had begun to fear for Kathy, but I replied,

"Oh that sounds like nothing to worry about, but how about you are you okay?"

"Yes I am fine, I just do my job at the bar, earn my money and live a quiet life" I had feared for Paula, but after talking to her I realized she was like Christy and a survivor, she would not get in anything too deep and stay away from bad situations. I needed to wrap things up as I had all I wanted, plus I had the gorgeous Putri waiting for me so I bid farewell to Paula, telling her to delete my number, but I would contact her in good time. She asked,

"Do you know where Kathy is then?" I had a good idea, but said,

"Not at this moment but when I find her I will let you know" she smiled and we bid farewell. I needed to set up a meeting involving Clifton, Gus and Charlie, and getting everyone to be introduced. I called Clifton first, he answered saying 'you are still alive then' I laughed and said that it seems that way. He laughed and asked how many had I killed, I told him none but we need to meet, same place tomorrow at 10am. He told me he would be there, I called Gus and Charlie passing on the same information, to which both said they would be there. Now I had lots of time to concentrate on Putri before I reveal my plan to deal with The Ular!

CHAPTER 11 MUSSALAH

After a fantastic night with Putri, it was time to get down to business. I told Putri that I would be back later so just relax, go for a swim and order some food. She told me she planned on going to the gym, swimming, then await my return. Good girl I thought and my heart was filled with joy, but I worried for her if anyone found out about me and her. I had a plan for that but other things needed taking care of first. We both went for some breakfast before I was due to leave. I ordered a Grab after breakfast kissed Putri with her tearing up again saying please be careful. Always my dear, I replied then left for Murphy's. When I got to Murphy's, I found Gus already there having a coffee.

"Always early big man as usual" I said,

"I needed to case the joint out first which took time" he replied, Gus is very efficient. I ordered a coffee then Charlie entered,

"Hi Charlie, let me introduce Gus, my partner" I announced, Charlie extended his hand to which Gus shook then said,

"Pleased to meet you pretty boy, are yee old enough to shave yet?" Charlie smiled replying with,

"Just, pity I can't say the same about you, old man!" Gus smiled and nodded, he likes Charlie which bodes well as we are all going to be working together.

"Yee wee cheeky fucker, come here and I will smack your arse!" was Gus's response smiling. The banter is always important to form a close team, which would continue if I don't jump in.

"Good, you have both made friends which is very important as we now look after each other!" Both men looking at me in bewilderment,

"All will be revealed when Special Agent Mathers arrives" I said. From that moment we all just talked with sarcasm and a liking for each other, then Clifton arrived. Again I introduced Gus with pleasantries passed from all involved, then Clifton asked me

"What's the plan Eraser?" Gus looked at me wide eyed with a 'what the fuck' look wondering who was Eraser,' later' I said to Gus and he nodded.

"Right to begin with, my meeting with Harper revealed him knowing he was being watched, so Clifton I don't believe he knows it's you guys but the little incident in Ciliwung will give him clues that it's not just a local gang watching him, so I was worried that the people you have on the inside are passing info to Harper and Naylor, as in this country money talks a lot, if you get my meaning!" I had begun and watched Clifton's reaction, I looked at Gus and he was miming 'Who is fucking Naylor?" I put my hand up to indicate to wait, I looked at Charlie who was digesting the Ciliwung incident and it was Charlie who spoke next,

"I thought the Ciliwung killings were gang related, so what really happened"

"They were as the news reported them Charlie, but let's just say we helped" I replied, I will tell Charlie what happened in good time but not here as other business was more important, then Clifton spoke,

"The people we have in the inside are bona fide legit and are on our side to fight for a greater good. They are also well compensated from the U.S Government as well as their country receiving lots of lucrative contracts keeping them amongst the rich countries of the world, so to answer your question, I don't see it being anyone we have on the inside passing information to Naylor and Co!" he looked angry as he spoke, I looked at Gus who was studying Clifton before looking at me and raising his eyebrows.

"Okay Clifton, I am no way accusing anyone of being disloyal, I am passing an observation from Harper who wanted me to know he was being watched. Maybe he thought it was me, I don't really care to be honest, all I care about is you and your team's safety Clifton, but if you are so adamant that no one can be turned by Naylor and his influential contacts then I am cool by that!" I replied trying to cool the situation down.

"No, don't take me the wrong way Eraser, I believe anyone can be bought if they are in a bad situation, but I am angry on the basis that our guys went through an intensive selection process with their families being well compensated and all backgrounds reset so no red flags would pop up leaving them vulnerable to outside evil. I also appreciate your concern for me and my team, but it's our problem and not yours so let's move on with the main business" Clifton is a straight as dye type of guy who I respected enormously, and I totally agree that all precautions would have been taken by the Americans for their operation. However, Clifton was right in saying anyone can be bought, so I worried for Clifton and hoped he was right about his people on the inside. He was also correct about the important business, so I relayed my plan to all,

"We are tasked to exterminate Mussalah so this is how we will do it, I want to make it look like a sloppy gang hit and not a professional hit that would create more questions than answers. So Clifton you need to supply me with a clean Glock then me and Gus will steal a motorbike then drive by old Snaky in his car, where I will shoot him through the window all with head shots and hopefully on his tongue. We will then ride to Depok, burn the bike, then rendezvous with Charlie who will be waiting in an arranged place with an unmarked vehicle to bring us back here Murphy's to hand you the gun back to destroy. Job done Mission complete and payment complete. It will look like a gang hit that has escalated to the streets of Jakarta." I looked at Gus who just put his thumb up in the air to me, but Charlie looked like he had shit his pants, I need to work on him, I thought. Clifton replied,

"Excellent plan James, I will relay everything to Ms. Page who will approve I have no doubt and I will get you the gun but give me some time with that"

"No problem Special Agent, but don't take too long as I need to return to England to wrap up the case I am working on" I replied, I wanted to strike before Mussalah got wind of a hit on him, which would result in extra security for himself and a drive by shooting being cancelled.

"Can we keep this to ourselves please, that means just the people here and your Page lady!" announced Gus, good man always thinking. Clifton replied,

"This is all hush hush I can assure you all and Eraser next time I contact you I will have the gun, so its bye from me, good luck fellas" Clifton would arrange what we needed and until then me and Gus need to do reconnaissance on Mussalah then pick our area to strike, I just need one more day with Putri before we put our plan together. Clifton left then Gus said tell me about Naylor then all about our payment. I relayed everything to Gus informing him that we are both being paid by the Yanks to help remove a parasite only for another to emerge from the shadows. He asked about Christy and I told him all about her and how fond I had become on her, he said he was looking forward to meeting her. Then Charlie jumped in saying that without permission from London he could not be part of the mission, I reassured Charlie that London is fully aware and compliant about our execution of Mussalah and absolutely no connection to the UK would be discovered. Charlie said I am employed by the British Intelligent Service so there is your connection. Gus butted in telling Charlie to calm down as his only involvement is to give 2 lost British tourists a lift to Jakarta and that's all he knows. Charlie wasn't convinced, so I said to him to resign his post and officially work for me. I need to think about things was Charlie's response. I was happy with that and wanted Charlie on board as he was a good guy and intelligent or smarter than me and Gus. Charlie said he would contact me in a day to let me know his decision, I said fine but don't talk about this to anyone please. He saluted put his right hand on his heart saying 'For Eraser and country' then walked out of the bar. Gus looked at me and said

"He will be in then and what's with the Eraser?"

"I think so my friend but in what capacity I don't know, it's an American thing Fraser the Eraser".

"Good, I like him, fucking crazy Yanks" replied Gus, we need to watch Ular's movements, follow his car and decide when would be the best time to strike. I like the gun coming from the Yanks leaving no trace to us or our contacts, plus giving them it back clean leaves us a million miles from it. Yes it does but Clifton knows that also so to continue with the plan means he is fully on board regardless. He is a top man Gus, who saved my life in Ciliwung, so I owe him."

"Aye, when were you going to tell me about that, you wee fucker, doing things without me?" I was waiting for Gus to have a go at me about that and knew it was coming,

"You were watching out for Putri and I can talk to a woman alone, just things got out of hand with a perp getting his head blew open while he held a gun to my head" I responded to Gus.

"You Crazy Geordie bastard, never again, we are partners and do everything together from now on, okay fucker?" Gus was annoyed so I just agreed. I told Gus to give me a day with Putri then we would start with tracking Mussalah. He said okay and he would look out for a powerful bike to claim, not one of the hair dryers that all the locals ride. Gus was as close to me as a family and we both cared for each other in our own special ways. I needed to get back to Putri but before that I had to call a very special person.

"Hello, is that James?" came the sexy voice on the other end of the phone,

"Hello Christy, are you okay?" I replied

"Well I am still in this hotel listening to whores getting fucked from every room" she declared,

"Good girl, as long as it's not you I have some good news, I will send you enough money to enroll on your course and to get through college without selling your body anymore" I told her, I heard a cheer then,

"OOH thank you James, I really love you and I won't let you down ever" said Christy, with conviction

"I will be coming back to Singapore soon and I want you to meet my partner who lives there and who will help you while I am away" I told her

"You mean you are leaving, I am so unhappy now" she said very sadly

"It's the nature of my job Christy but I will be back to keep an eye on you" I replied laughing,

"So you won't be leaving me then James, whoop woo!" she said with glee,

"Never Christy, you are my family now and will always have a place in my heart" I said meaning every word,

"James Fraser I will love you forever" replied Christy

"I love you too Christy, see you soon" I loved Christy like a family member because I was proud of her and what she had done to survive. She might be wanted for murder and theft in her home country but that was irrelevant to me as she saw a way out from her nightmare and had the balls to carry out her plan, she also ridded the world of a parasite who should have protected her instead of degrading her. I needed to get back to Putri and enjoy our freedom together while it lasted. I spent some magical moments with Putri eating in nice restaurants, shopping in malls, swimming, making love many times in the next few days. I felt alive, elated and totally in love, it was a wonderful time that would end soon. As I thought how good a normal life feels my phone rang, it was Gus and he said we need to start planning Fraze time is not our friend. I agreed and arranged to meet Gus outside my hotel later. I needed to break the news to Putri that I was returning to England, but would be back for her. I had planned on placing Putri with Gus in Singapore until I got back. I hoped she would agree. I broke the news to Putri who broke down and cried uncontrollably, she said I wouldn't return, but I assured her I would. I told her I wanted to marry her which changed the mood as she leapt at me embracing me saying yes I want to be your wife. Wow, I thought, amazing. I told her we would go out tonight with Gus my partner as he is the closest thing to family for me and I also thought that Gus will babysit Putri in his home in Singapore when I tell him tonight. She was ecstatic and so was I to be honest, I loved this lady with all my heart, which made me think of Roy and how he felt for Kathy. I told Putri that I was doing some business with Gus before we returned and all go out together to Loewy's. She was excited and said she couldn't wait. Gus texted saying he was 'outside waiting, red car, Toyota Impreza'. 'I replied coming now'. I got in the car and told Gus about our plans tonight, with Putri, He was flabbergasted and said, I will ask her about her sister tonight. I laughed, and then he said

"I have been watching The Ular for the past 2 days and he is very predictable, he always does the same things at the same time, he is either stupid or super confident no one will attack him." Always efficient is Gus I was glad he was on my side,

"I am going for stupid, which will make killing him easy" I replied

"We are going to the Government office in Senayan as he goes there every day around this time, then we will follow his car selecting where to hit him, with our getaway clear." Said Gus

"Sounds like a plan" I said. We then made small talk until we arrived at the location. We parked so we could view the entrance/exit and waited. It wasn't long when Snaky emerged from the building, poking his tongue in and out, the disgusting bastard.

"He will get in the black limo waiting over there, just him in the back with 2 subjects in the front." Gus pointed out to me, he was right and we watched the car pull out before we followed keeping at least 2 cars between us and a million bikes, it was Jakarta the city of bikes! Gus said

"He will head to Menteng to the ILGR Project Office, be there for a couple of hours before going to Blok M and Top Gun bar. We will follow as he takes the same route all the time" we didn't care what he was up to but had a good guess at what, we needed to find an ideal place to take him out. The roads to Menteng where heaving with traffic so for me it wasn't ideal. After waiting for him to come out of Project Office we followed him to Blok M. The roads were much better although heavy traffic there was a clear getaway on a fast bike and also if we struck at this time the night was rolling in giving us extra cover as 2 people dressed all in black on a bike should not rouse too much interest. We both agreed that this area was our location for the hit. We just needed to plan our getaway route to Depok which is outside of Jakarta. Gus told me he was planning on stealing a bike tomorrow and getting a good feel for it plus planning the escape route and driving it to see how long it would take to get to Depok. Again I agreed and just let him do his thing as I had full confidence in him. We continued following Snaky to Blok M before driving away and back to my hotel. Gus dropped me off saying he would meet me around 8pm in Loewys. I made my way back to Putri and a hot shower.

I was still being careful for Putri's sake and decided to walk to Loewy's which was about 10–15mins away. There was plenty of people walking in this area so we blended in well. We got to the restaurant got a table against the wall and waited for Gus. I had also brought my gun with me unknowing to Putri and I am sure Gus will have his. Gus arrived and after the introduction got on with Putri asking her many times if she had a sister. My phone pinged, it was Clifton, and he needed to meet me to give me a present. The fun was about to start. I said to Gus, after looking at my phone,

"Two days big man" he nodded and smiled. However, Putri said

"What's in two days?" I replied it's a secret honey, but you will be very happy about it. She giggled and said

"Can't wait"

"In the meantime sweetheart I want to make things official between us so please can I marry you?" as I got on one knee and handed her a plastic ring from a crackerjack box,

"Yes of Course" she screamed in delight with the full restaurant joining in with applause, and Gus looking at me with devilness. I told her we would shop in the morning for a real ring but she said okay but this will always be my favorite ring. We continued our night before Gus said he had to leave. We shook and said to each other see you soon. I wanted to get the future Mrs. Fraser back to the hotel to seal our engagement so I ordered a Grab and we left.

We had a fantastic night together before we got ready to shop in the morning. My phone rang while having breakfast, it was Charlie,

"Hello"

"I'm in, I am in Depok now just looking for our rendezvous point, there are some abandoned garages near the University of Indonesia with a lot of waste ground. It's ideal plus we can burn the bike and fuck off sharpish" he declared, good man I knew he would come round. Charlie is a stickler for authority but he also sees the big picture like me and Gus. He will be a welcome addition to our team.

"Brilliant Charlie, I will talk to you soon and we will correspond our plan" I replied. Putri looked at me and said that sounded serious. I told her it was nothing and not to worry and just let's have a good day together. She smiled, and looked happy. I needed to contact Gus so we can finalize our plan but I must do it away from Putri. We both went to the mall by a Grab, we had a wonderful day with Putri selecting a very nice decadent diamond ring that was as beautiful as her and very expensive for me. It's something I will need to get use to as I am discovering that Miss Delishus has expensive tastes. But I thought she is worth it! We had lunch together and I felt so happy with this lady beside me and I made a vow to myself to never put this beautiful lady in any danger, which means keeping her safe. While she was eating I excused myself to visit the toilet but called Gus to meet me at Murphy's tomorrow at 10 am were we will also meet Clifton and finalize our plan. I could now spend the rest of the day and night with Putri, which in respect could be the last day of my life, so I made the most of the day and her body. I had called Clifton when I got a moment alone to tell him about our meeting the next day reminding him to exchange presents. He laughed saying he will be there.

The morning after the night before I kissed Putri goodbye, skipped breakfast and told her to stay at the hotel until I came back. She looked worried but I reassured her I would be back later. I arrived at Murphy's with Gus already there having fully cased out the joint. I also saw a powerful Ducati motorbike parked outside. It was a lovely machine and I thought a crying shame to destroy it. I sat with Gus who just said

"It goes down today, no fucking around, get the gun and let's do it!" he was hyped up and in battle mode, I was happy about that as it meant no mistakes.

"Yes let's eradicate another parasite my friend" I replied. I was also becoming hyped with my adrenalin in full flow, then Clifton walked in saying,

"My favorite people I come bearing gifts!" he announced jovially, I looked in his eyes which had betrayed his confidence, so I asked him if everything was okay? He replied everything has the green light but I worry about the fallout when this scumbag is dead!"

"Don't Worry Special Agent, It will look like a gang hit which you will feed to your source on the inside who will feed it to the press, and then you get the added bonus of Naylor emerging from the shadows with I don't doubt Mr. Cordoba being extremely pissed off with all the publicity Mussalah and his operation will get. Just remember if you need us we are always available especially for you my American friend" I replied,

"That is reassuring Eraser and you are right, maybe I am getting soft as I age" he said but this time his eyes were brighter and he looked happier. He then handed me the package saying its

"Unmarked with a full magazine with untraceable bullets, make sure you don't miss!" he had become more determined now. I had no intention of missing and Mussalah was going to hell after I had unloaded enough bullets into his face, I thought. I told him that we would meet here the same time tomorrow where I could exchange my gift for him. He nodded stood and left. I looked at Gus he held up a bag and said

"Toilets to get changed."

"Wait lets contact Charlie first", I replied. I called Charlie to get into position today and to text me his location when he had arrived.

"No problems boss, everything is in order, plus I have a can full of kerosene for the bonfire!" Charlie replied and I was feeling even more content. Charlie was fully part of our team, good man. I went to the toilet to change into what Gus had got me, and it was a full black leather biking outfit with a very handy zipped chest pocket for my new present. I put my clothes into the back pack the black outfit came from and went back to Gus, who said my turn now. We both left found a bin and threw both backpacks into a bin before going to the bike and finding our full faced helmets with blacked out visor on. Gus had also got some coms so we could speak to each other quietly so we placed them in our ears before putting our helmets on.

"Check, Snake 1" said Gus

"Loud and clear Snake 2" Gus Raised his thumb, started the bike and we were away,

"We find Mussalah, watch him, follow him then strike" Gus announced, He was handling the bike like a professional racer and it was exhilarating. Knowing Gus he would have stolen the bike then raced it around the streets to familiarize himself fully with the bike, He was an excellent partner whom I would gladly put my whole life into his full hands. I felt me phone ping while riding pillion behind Gus and I knew we were nearing Mussalah's first drop off. I said to Gus.

"Let's stop and wait for Snaky to emerge, I have a message"

Okay nearly there we will stop so we can view our subject" replied Gus. We spotted his car outside the usual venue for his drop, stopped and looked at the message, it was from Charlie with his location. I replied with a thumbs up emoji. We waited for Snaky to emerge, Which he did, however, got in his car after looking around, he must be suspicious I thought, but even if he has been tipped off, he won't expect to be hit by a passing bike. I was not aborting, Gus must have thought the same but said,

"Let's continue and fucking rid the world of this depravity"

"Loud and clear" I replied we followed from a distance and watched him stop for his last drop. We watched him go inside and waited. We were very close now. He was inside for the usual length of time then once again he emerged looking around and up at the buildings around him, I thought he has definitely been warned his life was in danger, but he never knew how it was going to end. I thought of the Yank's sources and felt one had been turned. Still we would not abort, it was now or never, and then Gus said,

"It's time Fraze, let's get this on" we watched Mussalah drive off then we followed, I felt for the gun, I had already checked it and it had been cleaned, greased and ready to use. I felt a certain comfort feeling it near my chest. We had got to the area of our hit and we were in luck as traffic had backed up to a near standstill but not for bikes. Gus slowly pulled towards Snaky's car and when level, I took the gun out and shot once through the window. It shattered and I looked at Snaky. I had hit him in the face but his eyes were moving so

I slotted him 3 more times with one aimed at his disgusting tongue in his mouth. My last shot was a head shot which blew the back of his head out. I looked at the 2 Hench men in the front, the driver had looked around but the passenger had went forward holding his head in his hands. I said calmly,

"Done, deceased, let's go!" then Gus accelerated away zig zagging through the traffic very skillfully, I looked back and saw car doors opening with people getting out of their cars to look at the carnage in Snaky's car. I felt nothing but satisfaction that that piece of shit could not peddle his poison and destroy normal people's lives anymore. Gus then said,

"Classy Fraze, it's been a pleasure" I replied saying

"Let's get to Charlie in good time" he put his thumb up and we accelerated away. The bike was an amazing ride which with my adrenaline already at a high rate made it feel like I was in a TT race.

We got to Charlie in good time. The location was perfect with waste ground all around and Charlie inside abandoned garages and probably houses knowing how people live here. We were out of sight so we parked the bike took off our leathers and helmets, I washed the gun with kerosene then wrapped in some old cloth never to touch it again, I had arranged for Charlie to have a change of clothes for me and Gus which he came up trumps with, I poured the kerosene over the bike, leathers and helmets then set them all alight. We had changed and got in the car Charlie had acquired. Job complete now we had to get rid of the gun then make ourselves invisible again. On the way back to Central Jakarta, we talked normally as if nothing had happened then Charlie said,

"I resigned my post, yesterday. Dont get me wrong I loved my job but it was restrictive with rules and regulations, which made life for me at times unbearable, so although when meeting you guys, some of the stuff you do affected me, but then I saw that you were fighting evil with evil, to achieve the greater good, which appealed to me as the bad guys who prey on the weak and vulnerable are eradicated which makes me feel happy inside. You mentioned to me that I was part of your team James, So now I need a job and want to be very much part of your team" Gus from the back seat grabbed Charlie around his neck and kissed him on his head, saying,

"Good man, welcome on board"

"Gus, he is driving take it easy" I said and Gus let go laughing. I responded to Charlie,

"All will be revealed very soon Charlie boy, but let's finish this first. If you resigned who did you tell?" I asked

"Stella Mathews" he replied,

"Fuck! her pants would have exploded at that news" I said laughing and Charlie nodded laughing also.

"Gus, I want you and Charlie to go back to Singapore and your home tonight, from Halim, I will join you as soon as my meeting with Clifton is over and I will be with Putri" I announced, with Charlie responding saying he likes Singapore.

"Wait till you see were Gus lives!" I replied, with Gus laughing. Drop me at the Ritz-Carlton please Charlie the get yourself ready to move with Gus.

"Aye-Aye sir" he said

"Gus I will contact you when I arrive tomorrow afternoon in Singapore" I said

"The Old Monk will be waiting big man" replied Gus, I laughed and gave him the thumbs up. I now had to break the news to Putri that she was moving to Singapore and away from her life here in Jakarta I thought. I got to our room, kissed Putri and went to shower all the shit of today off me, then had amazing sex with Miss. Delishus. I was floating but also aware that the city would now be a very dangerous place to be. I turned on the news and saw that our 'job' had made the headlines, in fact it was a news flash with the CNN reporter at the scene saying

'Gang *violence exploded onto the main streets of Jakarta today, as Andre Mussalah was executed on a busy highway packed with commuters. He was the victim of a drive by shooting with reports stating, 2 subjects were driving a Ducati motorbike with the pillion passenger open firing into Mussalah's car shooting dead Mussalah with several shots then racing away at high speed. Mussalah is the most high profile victim of gang violence so far that has escalated out of control. Mussalah is believed to have connections far and wide across the world including drug cartels in Columbia and Europe. Police have iterated that the public need not be concerned as the violence is concentrated on the local gangsters that dominate Jakarta. Police have also called upon all gangs to cease these senseless killings and to peacefully settle their arguments. As of yet no body has come forward to claim responsibility for the killings. Investigations however will continue to find the perpetrators of this latest killing.'*

Well that confirms we were successful, plus Clifton's sources seem to be working overtime. Putri was also watching the news, looking at me and saying

"Jakarta is becoming a no go zone for ordinary people" to which I replied,

"That is exactly why I am taking you to Singapore to live tomorrow" she screamed in delight shouting

"I love the shops there!" I bet you do Miss Onassis I thought.

I need to contact Christy and DCI Tom Croft but not on my phone, I had a burner phone spare, so called Christy telling her to meet me on Orchard Road outside of Jamie's Italian tomorrow, She screamed with delight until I told her she will be meeting Putri also, To which she replied in a disappointing voice,

"Can't really see a chance of a threesome there!" I laughed and said

"What happened to the new Christy that wouldn't let me down?"

"Sorry James, I am only joking, I can't wait to meet Putri" she said happily,

"Good girl, see you soon" I responded then rung off.

I then called DCI Croft away from Putri, I told him I would be back soon, and that he needs to look deeper into Coombes and Centrepoint College. I gave him my reasons saying check if any other girls have gone missing from that college and that I want to speak to Coombes with himself present at his home so please arrange a warrant for that. Croft replied

"I take it you haven't found Kathy, but why the interest in Coombes?

"I need to check the video of Kathy at the bus stop as something initially bothered me about it and I want to take a fresh look to see what, plus Coombes has popped up with Kathy's friend mentioning him" I explained

"We investigated Coombes who came up clean, James, so why the warrant? Croft replied,

"I will tell you when I see you" I responded. With Kathy mentioning being the centre of attention by shit breath Coombes, she must have thought it was important so I aimed to interview Mr. Coombes when back in the UK. I might be wrong but it might be significant in the discovery of Kathy's whereabouts. I returned to Putri and I decided to stay in our room for the night readying for Singapore the next day. Besides I didn't want to go out around Jakarta with the city in turmoil. It's safer in the room with the delightful Miss. Delishus, I thought. We spent a very eventful night together then in the morning I told her I had a meeting to attend before returning for our flight to Singapore. I had booked the flight from Halim again, to avoid the glare of cameras at Soekarno-Hatta. I would tell Putri I preferred this smaller airport as the airlines involved were safer. She said okay but not to be too long then asked what she needed to do about her apartment if she was going to live in Singapore, I told her to just keep it. It would come in useful one day I thought. I left for my meeting with Clifton carrying my gift for him.

I arrived at Murphy's with Clifton already inside, he greeted me with,

"Eraser, well done, we have picked up lots of chatter since the demise of Mussalah between Naylor and Cordoba plus an unnamed subject in Europe. You have stirred a hornet's nest my friend. I also have a message from Ms. Page, congratulations and thank you on your operation, the $2 million is on its way to your new bank account as we speak." Thelma kept her side of the deal, perfect.

"Hopefully your target Naylor will reveal himself soon. I need to tell you something Clifton, be very careful with your sources because Musallah was aware he was a target, which could only come from the inside. He was just too arrogant to think it was happening. Just be certain about your sources and who you tell anything please Clifton"

I told him with concern. I was sure that Mussalah knew he was in danger plus Harper was aware of being watched which made me sure there was a mole in the camp. Clifton looked cool about it all but if it was me I would be looking at every source and seeing if anything had changed. However, it's not my business as my business was executed to plan. As I got up to leave Clifton stopped me and said,

"One more message from Ms. Page keep your phone open as she will be using you again for sure" responded Clifton, which I fully expected as the world is being filled with bad people making lots of money out of misery. I and my team will be ready for anything I thought then replied,

"I will be ready for anything and Ms. Page can sleep comfortably on a night knowing we are ready to respond to her call." I was serious, I am no white knight but the thought of scum and vermin slowly destroying the good people of the World totally pissed me off, making me determined to wipe the fuckers out. It was time to leave as I needed to catch a flight so I said to Clifton,

"Until we meet again, stay safe my American friend"

"I reciprocate that Eraser and I am sure it won't be long before we meet again, take care my good friend". And with that I was gone.

CHAPTER 11 SINGAPORE

On the way back to pick up Putri, I had thought about her huge commitment she was taking to be with me, so I decided to tell her what I did for a living and that she was in real danger being with me. She deserved to know so she could at this critical time in our relationship walkaway and continue her life without the knowledge she could be hurt or killed at anytime. I sat her down and revealed everything to her telling her I worked for intelligence agencies as well as ordinary people with my job putting me in the spotlight of evil people who would take away my nearest and dearest to get to me I told her I would keep her safe and give my life for her as I loved her so much. She eventually looked at me with tears in her eyes saying,

"I don't care what you do James I only care about you, you have given me a reason to live, you make me so happy and I cannot imagine a life without you, plus your sex is amazing" with a cute laugh as she said the last part, I was bursting with happiness inside replying,

"My sex is amazing because you are amazing my love, I will love you forever and I will never be far from you as you own my heart" I meant every last word and I had never felt so much love for someone, she was everything to me and more. With that we headed to the airport and while on our flight to Singapore I told her about Christy before she actually meets her. I told Putri that I love Christy like she is my family and I am proud of how she has defeated adversary. I think Putri and Christy will get on fine, I hope!

We landed in Singapore and I was James Fraser, However, through bad luck I got the same immigration officer who was a Newcastle fan. He looked at me before seeing my passport and said, it *was nice to see you again Mr. Beardsley'* Shit. I thought then rummaged through my back pack for Beardsley's passport. Putri just looked at me and smiled. *'It's good to be back sir'* I responded. We both went to the taxi rank after collecting our bags, I called Gus letting him know I would be with him soon, with two special guests, he replied that he was there with Charlie waiting in anticipation. I called Christy to get to the pick-up point as I was on my way. She yelped a sexy cry, *'see you soon James.* 'On arrival to pick up Christy I told Putri to stay in the taxi as I went to greet Christy. She was wearing a skin tight black dress that made her look stunning, she saw me and ran towards me leaping at me as I caught her she had wrapped her legs around my waist and arms around my neck then just kissed my face continuously.

"Christy, enough, Putri is in the car!" I shouted at her,

"Are you not pleased to see me James?" she questioned.

"Of course I am but not like we are lovers sweetheart, my future wife is watching and probably wondering what is going on!" I replied.

"Let me meet the lucky Putri!" she let go and unstraddled me and walked off towards the taxi, I was smiling and shaking my head at the same time. I got her bags and caught up to her,

"Let me introduce you please Christy" I proclaimed,

"Okay James, go ahead" I opened the taxi door and said to Putri, meet the wonderful Christy. Putri extended her hand and said to Christy,

"Wow you are very lively and beautiful, pleased to meet you" Christy was stood still with her eyes wide staring at Putri, then shook her hand saying,

"Oh my God you are truly stunning, no wonder James would not fuck me!" I laughed uncomfortably, looking at Putri who was smiling but shooting daggers at me with her eyes. She said to Christy

"Please get in and tell me more" shit, perhaps not I thought and said to Christy,

"Remember the new Christy please be careful" with Christy laughing then winking at me saying,

"I have nothing to tell apart from James is the most special man I have ever met and he is a huge guy!" which she found hilarious, I didn't, but Putri looked at me with a knowing look nodding her head. Even the taxi driver had forgot to drive as he listened to Christy and turned to me putting his finger across his neck with a nod to Putri's direction. I told him were Gus lived and said please hurry. Christy and Putri were talking like they had knew each other for years, but the conversation was all about me, which was making me very worried.

We arrived at Gus's place with me still alive thank fuck. I got out and noticed the house even more now, there was CCTV cameras everywhere plus I noticed motion detectors and knowing Gus he will have a small armory stashed somewhere. It was like Fort Knox which gave me immense comfort, we entered with Gus showing us to a massive living room asking if anyone would like a drink. I said

"Yes can I have the full bottle of rum please" with Gus looking at my face and smiling with a knowing grin. I said to the ladies this is Charlie to which Putri nodded and said hello, but Christy was stood with her mouth wide open staring at Charlie, I looked at Charlie and his eyeballs were nearly on his cheeks, this could go very well I thought. Then Christy said to Charlie,

"Can I kiss you to check if you are real?" which we all smiled at but Charlie was dumb struck before replying,

"Hell yea, please do!" Christy hadn't waited for that response as she was at him in a flash kissing his face all over like she had done to me earlier.

"Christy, calm down we need to all talk first before you get a room" I said

"Fuck talking, let's get a room now handsome Charlie" So this is Christy said Gus, you are a little minx.

"I don't really know what that is but if Charlie knows he can tell me upstairs!" replied Christy

"Christy I will promise to tell you if you just let James speak first please" said Charlie. Good old Charlie I could see he was smitten with Christy and we all knew what Christy's intentions were! I was very happy for them both and they made a beautiful couple.

"Right down to business, due to our success in Jakarta we were paid into an offshore account were it will be divided between the three of us. What I am proposing is that we become a team to be hired at any time by Intelligent Agencies with no job refused. However, we need a legitimate business to hide behind so I am locating my private investigation business here in Singapore. We will have the very gorgeous Christy as our point of contact plus when she passes her law degree she will be our lawyer and also make sure that all investigated work is legal. On the P.I front we look for missing persons, search for scammers who have destroyed people's lives, even tail cheating wives or husbands if required. With the Intelligence business it will be myself contacted by the specific agencies which will involve putting ourselves in danger. Are we all in?" I announced, with Christy speaking first,

"So who is paying for me to pass a law degree?"

"I am" responded Gus

"Christy with your determination and desire to succeed you will pass with no problems. That I am sure of and that will make me very proud of you!" I proclaimed, to which Christy pealed herself off Charlie, walked over to me hugged me tight and whispered in my ear I love you. I hugged her back looking at Putri who had tears in her eyes before Christy then made her way to Gus and hugged him and kissed his forehead saying,

"You are a very nice man and I will not let you down" before returning to Charlie's side. I looked at Gus who was blushing and I thought I saw a tear in the corner of his eye, then he said,

"Young Christy I am sure you will not let me or anyone down but its yourself you should never let down, James sees something in you which I after just meeting you see the same thing, so welcome to the team and I can assure you that if pretty boy Charlie does not protect you I will" it was pure conviction from Gus which instead of talking Charlie just put his arm around Christy and hugged her tightly as Christy had broken down in tears. Putri had also went over to Christy to comfort her then said,

"What is my role in the team?" Which shocked me but I understood what she was trying to say, so I replied,

"You are the reason this team has been formed, you are my reason to live, you are the shining light that we all strive to keep lit, you are my world honey" to which Gus just pretended to gag by putting his fingers down his throat then looked at me saying,

"For fucks sake Fraze! Putri if you are part of James's world then you are a part of ours also, so all you do is keep fucking Fraze happy!" which was much better than my response to Putri. I then added,

"We will be purchasing a new office in the city with expensive advertising for our legitimate business with Gus tasked to find that and model it to our tastes, Charlie you will be our chief investigator with Christy running the whole show while she studies. Gus keep a keen eye on them, Putri we need to talk." Gus then announced,

"There are seven bedrooms in here so we can all live together until you find your own places to live and you 2 youngsters keep the fucking noise down!" To which Christy stopped crying stood up and grabbed Charlie's hand saying

"Come on, I want to eat you, let's go" and off up the stairs they went. Putri said to me,

"What's up honey?" it was time to tell them all but Putri was obviously the main one to tell,

"The case I am on needs closing so I need to return to England to hopefully do that, but I want you to stay here with Gus and Romeo and Juliet up there" I could see her beginning to get upset, so Gus got up grabbed my shoulder and said talk to me later before leaving the room…

"Are you coming back?" Putri asked

"Of course I am I told you what I think about you, plus my business is here now, I love you Putri, let's go and find a room" Putri had genuine fear in her eyes but nothing would keep me away from her and I would be back. We went upstairs found a very ornate room and made passionate love.

Later I found Gus and we sat down for a few rums, we talked about our future, with me telling him that the Yanks will keep feeding us and the Brits will use us mainly because we pinched golden balls upstairs from them so we will always have work. I also said with you being able to find scammers I think work worldwide will roll in as those fuckers are relentless. However, I said, we need to follow the legal route with that as we can't just execute them all although I would want to! Gus agreed and said that fucking Christy is a piece of work, good find Fraze, I like her a lot but not as much as pretty boy.

She made my stomach knot when I met her and I fell in love with her as family, nothing else, although it came close but I resisted I told him. Gus looked shocked and shook my hand before filling my glass back up.

"So back to England, for how long and when do you leave?" said Gus

"I am going back to wrap us this case for my clients sake, so hopefully about a week, and leaving tomorrow." I announced

"Miss. World upstairs will be upset but I will watch over her for you, don't worry about her Fraze" I had total Faith in Gus watching over not just Putri but the young lovers who will all live together ensuring total safety for all. I was probably at the happiest point of my life at this moment as these people were the closest I have ever been to anyone in my life. I vowed to protect each and every one of them and I looked forward to watching us all grow together. With Putri she had melted my heart and gave me the love I had never been able to find, she was my complete world. However, I had to leave her alone which was tearing me apart and no doubt her but I had to return for Roy's sake who essentially gave me the chance to meet Putri while I searched for his Kathy. I really hope to find Kathy and reunite her with Roy. My trip back home will give me that answer. Me and Gus drank more rum talking shit as usual when Putri joined us then the two lovebirds made their way down, both looking extremely pleased with themselves.

"So who threw the bucket off cold water over you two then?" asked Gus, Christy looked puzzled but Charlie chuckled and said,

"We needed a drink" Charlie was a good guy who would treat Christy with dignity and respect. However, I hope he never introduces her to his very posh parents as they will have a cardiac! I looked at Christy and she was glowing, I think she had finally felt what loving sex was like. She looked across to me and Putri, walked over and sat next to me then whispered in my ear, thank you Mr. James I wish you were my father! I was touched and emotional, but just looked at her and smiled with a wink. She joined her new partner and we all talked and drank rum.

I had booked my flight for tomorrow night arriving in the UK the evening after. I thought I should speak to Stella and Wallace before returning to the North East. I woke the next morning next to Putri and watched her sleep. I was amazed at how beautiful she was and I felt a huge void inside of me to be leaving her even if it was for a brief period. I kissed her on the forehead and got up.

"Were you just going to leave without making love to me?" came a sweet voice from the bed

"Not a chance" I replied and jumped back in with her. It was frantic, passionate and loving sex which made me long for more, but I needed to shower and pack so we kissed and got up. While I showered she told me to call her at least twice a day to which I agreed. I met everyone for breakfast downstairs with Gus asking what our new business will be called, I replied,

"Eraser Investigations" with everyone laughing and I was thinking about Clifton and smiling.

"Excellent!" was the unanimous shout from all. So there we go our new business will soon be up and running.

CHAPTER 12 STELLA

When I got to the airport I called Stella to arrange a meeting at MI6 HQ. She wanted to talk but I cut her off saying my line is not secure talk soon. I arrived in London the next evening, booked into a hotel, and then called Croft. I told him I would meet him at the station in 2 days. He replied saying no problem. Looking forward to talking again. The next day I went to Stella's HQ were I was met by a very young lady who escorted me to Stella's office. She was sat there with Peter Wallace and she passed pleasantries with me. I was still in jet lag mode so had no time for my childish humor. I said,

"Mussalah is deceased, his operation has been disrupted and the gangsters got away"

"All very good James but we still have to deal with our Government officials questioning us to see if we had organized the hit" said Stella sternly

"Easy answer No it wasn't, so what's the problem?" I replied, she was masking her anger which could only be because she was gazumped and ignored by Thelma Page I thought. Then Wallace spoke,

"It's all very well that your mission went to plan but the big picture for us James is if it didn't our partners across the pond would have dumped everything onto us and washed their hands with you" I knew all that which is why everything I do is a risk but so does Wallace so there must be something else they aren't telling me,

"You and me both know the risks and recriminations so why are you so concerned?" I asked curiously

"We were trying to turn Mussalah and we were close but the Yanks wanted him dead. We felt he would be more useful working for us then dead." Explained Wallace, which shocked me,

"I thought we didn't negotiate with terrorists?" I announced.

"He was a drug dealer James, his product is being peddled on the streets of the UK" responded Wallace, now I get it I was to disrupt his operation as a warning to him that we could get to him anytime we wanted, so talk to us or else, I thought.

"Well now I understand but Mussalah is just a monkey whereas the Yanks wanted the organ grinder. He was not the big player and you are foolish to think you could have trusted him!" I said with anger in my voice.

"Maybe you are right James and Ms. Mathews here struck a bargain with Ms. Page, to save some face and to be part of the bigger picture. Because the Americans target is English Stella demanded to be part of the action in apprehending him." Good little Stella, that rigid backbone was not for bending, but I said

"I don't think they want Naylor arrested if I am being honest and I am expecting that job!" I announced. Stella replied

"We don't care if he comes back in lots of plastic bags I told Ms. Page that if they use you again we want a part of it and we want Naylor here in whatever capacity." Well this is going better than I thought and Stella has revealed a ruthless streak in her armor, I admired her guts. I responded,

"That's fine by me I have my team now and we are ready for orders from all sides which we will carry out efficiently and thoroughly as you are aware of my methods Stella!" her face went back into stern mode and she turned to Wallace,

"I know your capabilities James and so does Stella, we cannot keep denying your actions to our Superiors while the Americans celebrate. It doesn't look good and it makes us look like amateurs as our own military personnel are working for other nations, we or Stella demanded to be a big part in their plans plus we can help you James" it's why I liked Wallace he never hid behind innuendo's he told it how it was, he didn't want the UK look like runners up in an egg and spoon race so demanded a piece of the action. That was fine by me as the Yanks had more enemies than us so more work would come my way with MI6 helping in the background. It was a win win for me and my team.

"Brilliant Peter and Stella, I admire your courage to stand up for yourself and your country, you can rest assured that me and my team will always be at your service!" I said, Stella replied

"Your team, does it consist of one of my recently resigned officers by any chance?"

"It certainly does as he told me he prefers my methods rather than wasting time with legalities. And he is excellent!" Wallace grinned and said

"That's fine James, just look after him please" I intend to do that and also train him to mine and Gus's standard. Stella then spoke,

"By the way have you found Kathy Mckray? Good question which deserves a good answer,

"No" Stella raised her eyebrows waiting for more

"I am meeting with DCI Croft tomorrow with the hope of wrapping this case up very soon" I didn't have much more to tell her yet so I said,

"Are we still getting paid for our services?" I waited in anticipation,

"Yes of course, you are proving to be very useful to us James so you will be paid accordingly" said Stella,

"Thank you Stella, just to let you know, you look stunning today and if I wasn't meeting Croft tomorrow I would escort you for drinks tonight" I said with sarcasm, well I had to have one crack at melting her pants.

"That's a pity James as my boyfriend would be wondering where I was, but thanks for asking and maybe another time?" she said with a smile and hint of sarcasm, I liked Stella even more.

CHAPTER 13 CENTREPOINT

I decided to go back to my home town by train which takes around 4 hours, so plenty of time to think and focus on Kathy. I also thought about Stella who on the exterior showed her English stiff upper lip but on the interior was ruthless, determined and feisty. I was shocked by her telling me she had a boyfriend and could imagine he was a la de da company director or CEO of a bank, to go with her image. I then pictured her having sex with him and imagined she would dominate proceedings which would be coordinated so she could stop every now and then to put her hair right, or maybe she is the total opposite and likes to be dominated and is wild and adventurous, this thought made James jnr twitch which reminded me to call Putri. To hear her voice made me warm inside and we talked until I was nearly home. I wanted to go to my apartment and sleep in my own bed to defeat the jet lag. On arrival at my place I headed for the bed and just dropped in totally shattered. The next morning I woke feeling fresh and ready to discover what happened to Kathy.

I got to the police station in good time with Croft coming to get me and taking me to his office.

"I take it I am not dangerous anymore as I get the Royal treatment today" I said to Croft as I sat in a nice comfy chair in his office. Croft had seated behind his desk which was very tidy and neatly arranged.

"Oh you are dangerous James but I think I am not your enemy so I will survive today" Croft replied with a smile. Then straight to business,

"Why all the sudden interest in Coombes?" he questioned

"As you will be aware if you ever spoke to him, his breath smells of a thousand buffalo farts, so when I questioned Kathy's friend

Paula, she told me that someone with bad breath was paying too much attention to Kathy, so it has to be Coombes" I answered

"Besides I need to look once more at the last video of Kathy because something bothered me about it which I will know when viewed again"

"Okay let's take a look now before I give you what we found out" replied Croft, I was now getting curious *what we found* hmmm! Croft put the video on and we both watched. I saw Kathy at the bus stop then,

"There, freeze that! She looks up at something"

"It looks that way, but what?" responded Croft,

"My guess is someone she knows and they have stopped seeing her at the bus stop then offering her a lift, move the video on" I proclaimed, the video continued but almost immediately the bus arrived, stopped, and then moved away.

"It's just a presumption James, but I agree it looks like she knows someone" said Croft

"What if she didn't get on the bus? Hell that fucking driver couldn't remember her, but if she had got on he would have remembered as Kathy was a beautiful lady!" I announced, I was now convinced Kathy never got on the bus but went with the unknown 'friend'. But did she go voluntarily or was she forced? I relayed my thoughts to Croft who then told me what they had found,

"It seems feasible James but not enough to arrest someone. What we found after going through the records of that college was 9 years ago another woman disappeared, she was a Vietnamese student called Trang Hanh, and she was 21 and attended the college to complete her English language degree. Coombes wasn't her tutor but he was in charge of that department at the time. Trang had one more exam to complete her degree, but never showed up. The college investigated her disappearance even calling the police to investigate who went to her address, which had been emptied and left totally clean, so they presumed she went back home maybe because of an emergency. However, the officers on the case contacted her family who said they had not seen or heard from Trang for months." I was shocked and said

"Fucking Coombes is the prime suspect Tom, he must be stopped!" I wanted to rip the fucker's heart out, then Croft said,

"A month later, her family contacted the officers and told them Trang had been in touch saying she was in Thailand after meeting a nice man whom she was planning to marry, so the officers closed the case" Bullshit I thought then said,

"What a pile of shit Tom, Coombes could have sent that email plus Asian people do not get married without family present, it's that greasy haired fucker, he has killed her and now I think he has killed Kathy, I will make him wish he hadn't been born!" I was full of rage and now stood up when Croft spoke again,

"James calm down we have no evidence that Coombes is the perpetrator, Trang's family receive emails from Trang every 3 months. We checked Coombes computer and nothing was on it, he is squeaky clean, we checked his farm where he lives and we found no trace of Kathy or anyone else. His wife gives him a perfect alibi saying he was with her after he finished his shift at the college"

"I want to interview him at his fucking farm Tom, the bastard will have more than one computer plus his slut wife knows about him but is probably too scared to talk, I want to interview her also!" I replied

"James this is not a war zone where you can intimidate and torture suspects, if you interview him I will be with you and I will warn you that any violence or threats will be reported and acted upon." Proclaimed Croft, Fucking legal system is a joke! It allows dangerous villains like Coombes to walk free after committing illegal acts, I was fuming but had to agree to Crofts request.

"What does he farm" I asked Croft'

"Pigs, he breeds them, corn feeds them then sells them to a local butcher" very convenient I thought what else does he feed them? Pigs will eat anything, the fucker has thought of everything to get away with murder.

"Convenient" was all I replied with and Croft looked at me knowingly,

"I will arrange to interview him at his home, but remember James, he can have his solicitor present if he wants so stay calm, please" Croft said,

"He won't have his solicitor present as he is an arrogant bastard who thinks he has got away with murder and I bet his wife won't be present either!" I replied

"Okay James I will get it arranged, what are you going to do now?" he asked

"I am going to Centrepoint to speak to the ayatollah Sally Jenkins"

"James keep it legal and keep your temper with her!" Croft reminded me, I had no intention of losing my temper with that woman but I wanted to put some accusations to her and her policies to see her reaction.

I called ahead to arrange a meeting with Jenkins, she had agreed saying she was very busy so could only grant me 30 mins of her time. She is a piece of shit who thinks she is in charge of the country and not a fucking college that is potentially a breeding ground for villains, terrorists and murderers. I wanted to rip her throat out, I detested this woman! I met her at reception and she walked me to her office, then asked,

"What can I do for you Mr. Fraser?" I nearly replied throw yourself from the roof please, but instead said,

"Tell me about Trang Hanh"

"Trang!! She was a student here before my time who apparently disappeared before her final exam, which I find is very strange as by all accounts she was a model student and about to complete her degree with the highest standards" she said,

"So what do you think happened or do you know?" I asked

"There was reports she had met a man whom she fell in love with and decided to run away with him, as I told you I wasn't here at the time so I can't confirm those reports" she explained. I thought what an arrogant bitch she is basically saying that if she was here it wouldn't have happened, so I said

"You are here now and Kathy Mckray is still missing, so that makes two Asian women missing from your college!"

"What are you trying to say Mr. Fraser that I am in some way responsible for those two women disappearing?" She said in a fluster with her face reddening in anger,

"No but I have to ask the question now as you don't seem too bothered that the reputation of this college is tarnished" I responded,

"Mr. Fraser our college has a brilliant reputation and is regarded as an elite college with many of our students progressing into important careers" she had regained her arrogance, but I wasn't finished,

"The reputation your college has is because you don't publicize the fact two young women have gone missing or the fact you teach anyone to become a danger to our society! You bury all that under your achievements"

"I think we are finished now Mr. Fraser" she replied looking away from me

"You will be finished soon you arrogant bitch!" I responded

"How dare you, you uncouth man!" she screamed at me, which warranted an intelligent reply, so I said,

"Fuck off!" I left feeling satisfied and hoped that when I tip the press off about this college she finds herself in the gutter were she belongs.

I checked my phone when leaving the college and seen I had a voicemail. It was Croft and Coombes had agreed to meet us at 8pm tonight. I called Croft telling him I would pick him up at the station later.

When I got Croft he told me that Jenkins had complained about my behavior and that I was not allowed back into the college without a police officer present.

"Oh I feel wounded, fucking bitch, I will never return to that place anyway Tom" I said in response. Croft nodded his head and said to me

"Stay calm with Coombes when you speak to him or I will be forced to arrest you which I don't want to do. Off the record I think you are onto something with Coombes but stay focused with your questions" we drove in silence as I didn't respond.

We arrived at Coombes farm and as we drove up he was waiting at his door for us, no solicitor was present, he thought he didn't need one as he was innocent, I thought. He showed us into his living room and I asked,

"You alone or is your wife joining us?"

"It's just us Mr. Fraser as my wife has gone out with her friends" he said with confidence and I looked at Croft who looked at me knowingly, I said,

"Let's just relax and talk, not like an interview, just a conversation, is that okay with you Jim?" I wanted him to feel comfortable and untouchable,

"Yes that's fine, what do you want to talk about?" he was relaxing, so I watched him carefully when I said

"Trang Hanh and Kathy Mckray/Cuzon" he sat back and clasped both hands together becoming nervous. I watched all his traits to recognize his tell,

"I hardly knew Trang but Kathy was my student as I have told you before" he said but when he mentioned Trang he made a fist with his right hand, that was his tell.

"Okay, so in your capacity at the time did you ever have contact with Trang?"

"Well, yes I was the head of English and maths department" he was relaxed again

"How many times did you have contact with Trang?"

"It was a long time ago, so I can't remember" right fist made as he lied,

Did you find it strange that Trang would just leave all her hard work behind to run off with a man?"

"Yes it's why I reported it to the police, I thought she had wasted her whole life for love" he lied as his fist clenched harder

"How many computers do you own?"

"Just the one which I surrendered to the police for forensic investigation" another lie as his fist was clenched harder,

"Where were you the night Kathy went missing?" I was now in full flow and hitting him with questions to unbalance him,

"I was working late as Kathy just left my class before I left to come home" he had relaxed again,

"Do you pass the bus stop outside of the college on your way home?"

"No, I drive the other way home as it's quicker" he was now panicking as both fists clenched as I mentioned the bus stop,

"Why does your breath smell like shit?" I was getting irritated by this bastard and his lies so it was time to step up my questions,

"That's a very personal question Mr. Fraser and unfortunately I have a problem with my teeth" he lied again the greasy bastard,

"Why do you own a farm but only breed pigs?" I asked

"Because they are always on demand from butchers, so I feed them well to get the most money back"

"I thought it was because you abduct women, bring them here, probably rape them before you kill them then feed them to your fucking pigs!" I shouted,

"James that's enough!" shouted DCI Croft

"That's a disgusting accusation Mr. Fraser and one you have no proof to!" shit breath said with confidence, so in a flash I was at him with my right hand clamped on his throat and tightening as I shouted at him

"What was their last words you fucking freak?" then I felt Croft on me pulling my arm from his throat shouting,

"James let go it's me Tom" he was pleading with me while Coombes was writhing in agony. I let go and said to Coombes,

"What does it feel like you fucking murdering bastard?" he was coughing and shouting,

"I want him arresting for assault he is crazy!" looking at Croft, but Croft responded with,

"All I seen was you Mr. Coombes attack Mr. Fraser and he acted in self-defense" which was brilliant from Tom but Coombes wasn't finished,

"I will have your badge for this and you, you crazy fucker I will have you incarcerated" before I could respond, Croft said,

"Go ahead, but let me tell you this you fucking depraved son of a bitch, I believe you are responsible for the murders of Trang Hanh and Kathy Mckray, I do not have any evidence to convict you but until the day I die I will follow you and hound you until I do!"

Croft was a superstar and I wanted to high five him, but just said to Coombes,

"If he doesn't catch you the next time you meet me will be the last time you breathe your shit breath"

"Is that a threat Fraser? Shouted Coombes

"No it's a fucking promise you fucking warped monster!" I replied, then Croft said

"We are done here James lets go" and with that we left. When in the car I apologized to Croft for putting him in a bad situation, but he told me that he thought I was right and that Coombes was a serial killer who fed the bodies to the pigs then sold the pigs to butchers who sold the pork and remains of the victims to ordinary people destroying all evidence.

"He is as you said a monster and I will watch every move he makes until he slips up" said Croft,

"We need his secret computer then we can find the emails he sends to Trang's family" I replied

"It will be long gone now James plus we turned his farm upside down and found nothing" Said Croft disappointingly,

"He will keep trophies Tom, they all do, its finding where though, I bet his wife knows, but she must have a problem with her nose as his breath is awful"

"Yes it certainly is and how convenient his wife being out tonight"

"He thinks he has got away with the murders Tom, so what's next?" I asked

"Nothing, we watch him until he slips up but we make him aware we are hounding him" replied Croft,

"So in the meantime he walks around with his head held high while we know he is a murderer and the victim families have nothing but memories?" I said,

"That's it James until we can bring him to justice he has in respect got away for a double murder"

"Fucking justice my arse, only justice is my type!" I said with rage. But Tom looked at me saying,

"We live within the law of the land James otherwise it would be anarchy with lawlessness abound. We can't go around dishing out your type of Justice James we need to go through courts and adhere to the law. But before you respond, I kind of like your justice and a part of me did not want to pull you off that bastard" Croft was right we live in a civilized country with written laws that we abide by, but sometimes those laws don't serve all, so that's when I step in. However, I was pleased that Croft was on my side but he won't be next to me to see Roy Mckrays reaction when I break the news to him. I thought about Roy and wondered what I would tell him, I was dreading it.

CHAPTER 14 KATHY

I left it till the next morning to break the news to Roy. I had contacted him to tell him to ask his daughter to be with him, his response was desperation and I heard his voice break as he told me he would be waiting for me to break the news. When I arrived his daughter came out to greet me with sadness in her eyes. She looked at me and asked,

"Is she alive?" I just shook my head and she started to cry. I informed her to be strong for her father's sake. She nodded and took me inside. I looked at Roy and I could see he was preparing for the worst, he was distraught, his eyes were red and his hands were around his mouth. Roys daughter sat with him ready to comfort him so I didn't want to prolong the agony and said,

"Roy I am afraid Kathy will not be coming home" to which Roy let out a heartbreaking cry of

"Noooo!!!" I continued,

"I will tell you the truth Roy and some of it you will find it hard to understand, Kathy was being used as a drug mule by an evil Cartel Baron, the reason Kathy resorted to being a mule was to feed and protect her family. She had a good heart Roy. However, Kathy decided to take some of the drugs inside of her and used the money she received to find a life over here in this part of England. That's when she met you Roy and fell madly in love with you, so turning her back on her past to live a wonderful future with you. I spoke to her family and although they live in poverty Kathy sent them enough money to live happily and feed themselves. Kathy also secretly enrolled into a local college to learn a skill to enable her to earn her own money so she could send that home in the knowledge she would always be well off herself with the love of her life, you Roy. However, from my investigation, the drugs Baron in Indonesia located Kathy, got her abducted and killed her." Roy just kept crying and shouting

"Nooo she was as pure as snow, she would never do those things!" the truth really does hurt I thought, but continued,

"I believe that her body was burnt or buried somewhere in Indonesia, so I am sorry I could not bring her home for you Roy, But I can assure you that the Drug Baron will ply his trade no more" I had no intention of telling Roy about Coombes, as in his state he was capable of anything, he replied,

"Is the bastard dead?"

"Yes he is Roy, but don't focus on him, focus on the memories you had with Kathy, she told her family about you and how she had found true love, and you were a truly, wonderful man whom she worshipped" Roy was in deep pain but his daughter was helping him cope, I was happy about that, but feared for Roy's mental state and hoped he would pull through this abyss he is now in. I didn't want to stay around watching Roy torture himself, so I gave his daughter my number and told her to contact me anytime she felt the need, she thanked me for everything I had done for Roy and told me to take care. It was time for me to leave and plan my return to Putri and Singapore. I just couldn't help thinking I had failed Roy, but in reality before he contacted me Kathy was dead so I must stop beating myself up about it. I am sure there will be lots more adventures featuring heartbreak and glory for me to be part of but hopefully minus the heartbreak.

THE END

Thank you for reading *The Connection*, and I hope you enjoyed it. Look out for the next book in this series *The Connected* coming soon. That will be followed by *The Hyena* before the final explosive book in this series called *The Head of the Barbed Chain.*

ABOUT THE AUTHOR

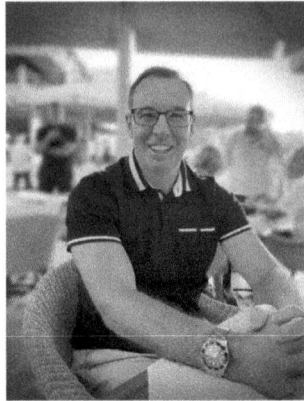

Dave resides in Hartlepool in England UK with his wife Melanie and his dog Noah. Dave was a very talented non-league footballer who is now an avid Newcastle United Fan. Dave is a retired oil and gas instructor/assessor who has worked on contracts all over the world gaining experience and knowledge of the places that appear in his books. Dave is a regular gym user, also spending his time walking his dog and writing. Dave suffered a stroke in 2019 and writes books to keep his mind active.

Milton Keynes UK
Ingram Content Group UK Ltd.
UKHW040020281223
435051UK00001B/56

9 798887 938912